Rob White is a fiction author, blogger, comic book collaborator and professional dreamer. Rob makes his home in Athens, Georgia, where he revels in the chaos and magic of living in a town full of artists and collaborates with other mad and beautiful souls as frequently as possible. The Pull was his first novel, begun at age fourteen in 1994, completed in 1999 and finally released in print edition in 2013. Its sequel, Home is Where the Monsters Are is the second in a series of five novels and a labor of nearly two decades of imagination.

To Brendon,

Follow Your Own Pull

ISBN-13 978-1493572373
ISBN-10 1493572377

http://followthepull.com/

Rob White

The Pull Volume 2

Home is Where the Monsters Are

Prologue

This world we live in is a strange one. The last year of my life was the strangest yet but I somehow know it only scratched the surface. Metal demons, a boy with no memory, a handful of young upstarts successfully standing against the most powerful man in America - perhaps the world.

Amazing things have happened to me since I met that masked boy with the green eyes and the pull inside of him. Amazing things have happened and I know without a doubt that amazing things are yet to come. Beautiful things. Terrible things. I know this because I dream about them.

Sometimes I wake up and remember. Other times I don't and carry with me the vague sense that something rich and powerful and ageless is stirring and we are all a part of it. That ageless power is what we call fate. It is more aware than we think, however. It calls to us. It directs us. It pulls us.

I don't yet know where it is pulling him. I know that question haunts him every day as The Pull grows stronger and louder and more insistent. It pulled him to Atlanta, and there he found other heroes and stood with them against monsters both real and figurative - the monsters without and the monsters within. Some were defeated. Others still attempt to claw their way out from within each of them. I feel that one of them in particular will soon come to face the monster within herself, and the others may suffer for it.

They are my friends and yet they feel like strangers to me. They feel like pictures in a book or words from a poem. I feel that way about myself sometimes too. There are things down that road coming for me as well. Will I become a hero like them? Or will I succumb to my own monsters, and fall before my own purple fire?

1

I've played a part in this story and I have parts yet to play but for now these chapters belong to them. Four heroes, each with a pull of their own. Each has a destiny and a monster to overcome. Each has a weapon they hold close and a dream of a future they will fight for. Without each other I have no doubt that each of them would fall, broken and alone - yet together they stand strong. Together they will change the world. In fact they've already begun to do so.

My name is Patricia. Like my brother, I sleep now. Like him, when I sleep I see the world for what it really is. I see the story of humanity. There will be loss in this tale; but there will also be triumph. I close my eyes...and turn the page.

1

She watched them from the corner of the room, her jaw clenched and her fists squeezing tightly around her staff. There was something about these guys that bothered her. Much more so than the average punks and wanna-be gangsters she had beaten up in the past. There was something about them that offended her more. They reminded her of something she would rather forget.

Melissa took a deep breath and tried to calm herself. Usually she welcomed the bloodlust. That shot of pure adrenaline filled her with a passion and joy she simply could not feel in any other part of her life. The motion, the action and reaction, the sounds of her fists, her feet, and her weapon smashing against bone, flesh and steel. It felt wonderful. Even the pain felt wonderful.

This did not feel wonderful. She wanted to get it over with, and that realization bothered her deeply.

There were about seventeen of them - some in robes, some in plain clothes. The ones that were dressed up looked like they had just come from a sci-fi convention. Lord of the Rings rejects. Servants of the Dark Lord.

That's what they were, really. They were cultists. Practitioners of some phony dark art under Raven's payroll. After some disappearances in the city, Nick had tracked the group down and discovered the names of two of them. Some digging, along with a little breaking and entering, had uncovered that these men were working under some top-secret project funded by RavenCorp. Melissa had never heard of Raven experimenting with the supernatural, but Jason seemed to think it may have something to do with Raven's mysterious "mentor" - a man referred to in Raven's files only as "DM."

No one knew the man's true name, and Melissa had never had the chance to meet him - a fact which she had always found odd, considering how often she was required to be in Raven's presence. Jason had seen him twice, and on both occasions he remembered feeling an overwhelming sense of discomfort, as if the man radiated it.

She took another deep breath, trying to keep the anger and discomfort in check. It was show time.

Six of the cultists, standing around a wooden table in the center of the gaping warehouse, turned as they heard the footsteps approach. They reached for their weapons in alarm and protest. One of them opened his mouth to yell a warning to the others.

Melissa, bearing an unnerving grin and carrying her six-foot-long staff slung above her shoulders, beat him to the punch.

"Howdy boys. Hope you don't mind if my friends and I join the party. We just get so upset when people decide to start the chanting and sacrificing without us."

The sight of the tall, athletic blonde entering the room surprised them out of their concentration. The men looked at each other nervously - each holding wicked curved knives in front of them.

"There are more of you?" one man asked with a nervous edge to his voice. These cultists were not trained fighters, after all - only part-time magicians who tried to inflict pain from afar.

"At least two," Melissa answered, her smile growing wider.

A low growl erupted from the shadows where Melissa had been hiding. The men's eyes widened as a large German Shepherd walked towards them, the fur on its back raised in a show of aggression, its teeth bared in anger.

"There's one," Melissa said.

"And here's another," came a voice from above.

The men looked up just in time to see the silver gleam of a curved sword and the moving shadow of a man dressed in black leap from the rafters. The masked man landed silently behind them. His dark brown hair hung over his forehead - his thin, lithe frame posed for action. He crouched low with his sword held to his side and his hazel-green eyes seeming to bore holes into their tainted souls.

"Shit, it's him!" one of them screamed, and then all hell broke loose.

4

Melissa, Nick, and Blitz were not alone. Stacy watched the fray erupt from the doorway. She felt a twinge of concern for her friends, but it did not last long. Sure, it was three against seventeen, but most of the cultists looked like they belonged more in their mom's basement rolling dice and arguing about dragons and orcs than trying to hold their own against two trained fighters and an angry dog. Still, one or two of them were kind of big....

Stacy shook her head and forced herself to put her maternal feelings aside. Sure, there were times when she felt like a mother looking after a group of dysfunctional children, but she knew she had to trust them. Nick especially would not have led them into a situation he didn't believe they could handle.

She held her crossbow trained in front of her as she made her way down the dimly lit hallway, searching for the door Nick had told her would be there. Behind that door were the victims of this particular cult. At least four men and women kidnapped from their homes and brought to an old warehouse in the industrial quarter of New Orleans for God knew what kind of terrible purpose.

Though after seeing some of the tables adorned with shackles and caked with what looked like dried blood in the other room, she thought she had an idea.

With Jason cutting off their escape and Nick and Melissa engaging the cultists themselves, it was Stacy's job to search for any surviving captives. She hated being given the easy job again, but she supposed it was what she was suited for.

Stacy froze as a hand clamped around her shoulder and a knife poked her in the ribs.

"My, if you aren't the beauty," came the voice of a scruffy and rather large cultist beside her. She cursed herself for not paying more attention.

Her long dark hair - bound in a pony tail, dark brown eyes and pale skin did cut a striking image in the dimly lit hallway.

"I'm going to have some fun with you," he said. She felt his breath move closer to her face.

"Have fun with this," she said, and whirled around, twisting out of his grasp and firing a crossbow bolt into his thigh.

The man screamed in pain. Stacy brought the butt of her crossbow across his temple with as much force as she could muster. He stumbled backwards, but did not fall. So she did it again.

He fell that time.

5

She looked down at him, her eyes wide. She felt like her heart was about to jump out of her chest.

"Asshole."

The door was right in front of her. It was big and old and wooden, with huge steel hinges and iron braces. It looked like a relic from the 1600s.

The bolt was unlocked. She didn't like the look of that.

Stacy threw open the door, aiming her weapon into the darkness just in case.

Then she lowered it, a look of defeat crossing her face.

"Oh no," she whimpered.

Melissa moved like an angry tornado. Her staff seemed to the cultists to be in eight places at once. She spun and kicked and occasionally threw a fist or an elbow into the face of a man who would soon need reconstructive surgery.

They were terrified of her - more so than they were of The Masked Hero. At least he was cutting them up and then moving on to the next man. The woman, on the other hand, just seemed to keep beating.

Her mind was no less furious than her movements. At first she had succeeded in losing herself in the familiar joy of battle, but eventually that discomfort, now bordering on panic, had begun creeping back.

And she knew why. Heaven help her, she knew exactly why.

Nick vaulted over the head of a man who had to have been six-and-a-half feet tall. He was probably the only cultist here of any real size, and for that Nick was grateful. He didn't need another Francis McElroy situation. Those bruises didn't go away for weeks.

He ran, jumped, rolled and slashed between seven men in alternating movements. Most of them were just putting up a token resistance, and none of them had landed a blow on him yet. He hoped it would stay that way. The wounds he was inflicting upon the men were minor at best, needing stitches to repair, if even that. Nick had learned to rely on simple scare tactics to win most fights, unlike Melissa, who seemed to take great pleasure in breaking every bone she could reach. Still, he had never seen her take a life.

As he stole glances at her between dodging and slashing, he wasn't sure if that record of hers would hold. She was fighting like a woman possessed. Her moves were reckless. Her defenses were wide open half the time - and her eyes bore a kind of rage and fear he found unnerving. She wasn't herself, and he was afraid it was getting worse as the frantic seconds ticked past.

It was in the middle of that reflection that Nick was hit in the back with a chair.

He stumbled forwards and managed to turn around in time to see the big guy he had recently jumped over swing a broken chair leg at him.

Crap, Nick thought. Maybe this wouldn't be as easy as he had thought.

Jason flung the small knife to the ground and walked quickly towards the sounds of battle in the warehouse. With every tire in the parking lot slashed, he knew any cultists lucky enough to sneak away from Nick and Melissa wouldn't be going very far.

Truth be told, he couldn't wait to join the battle. He hadn't had a real chance to vent his frustration in months. They weren't Raven, but these sadistic losers would have to do.

As he moved down the hallway, Jason's eyes narrowed beneath his dark glasses - glasses he wore constantly to remind himself of the darkness of his prior captivity by Jacob Raven. Jason was an imposing sight. He was the tallest of the four standing at six feet with a thickly muscled frame and dark skin beneath long unbound dreadlocks.

Something was wrong with the sounds he was hearing. It was Melissa. She didn't sound right. He was used to the grunts and screams she usually threw around during practice and combat, but this time…those screams sounded less exuberant and more…afraid.

Jason began to move faster, but then halted in his tracks as he saw a large shape move towards him from the dark end of the hallway. His chain dropped from his sleeve, and he prepared himself to use it.

Stacy emerged from the darkness, carrying someone along beside her.

"Oh my god," Jason exclaimed.

On Stacy's arm was a man who must have weighed close to ninety pounds. His emaciated form was covered in cuts and bruises and worst of all....

"His eyes...did they..."

"They sewed them shut," Stacy answered for him. "He was the only one still alive. I'm sorry, Jason. We didn't make it in time for the rest."

Jason's brow furrowed in anger. His zeal to join the fight had just grown exponentially.

"Get him out of here, I'll see to the...."

Stacy suddenly looked over into the doorway beside her - the entrance to the warehouse proper where the battle was taking place. Jason watched her swing her left arm around the man she was holding and her trigger finger squeeze on her crossbow in the blink of an eye.

He ran to the doorway to see what had happened just in time to see a large man hopping away from Nick with a crossbow bolt buried in his knee-cap.

Nick saluted them and then went back to mopping up what was left of the opponents on his side of the room.

There weren't many of them. Jason saw that most of them were crowded around Melissa.

"What's wrong with her?" Stacy asked.

Jason didn't know. His intuition in the hallway had been correct. She was swinging her staff wildly and barely looking at her enemies. Her eyes were wide and her teeth were bared. She looked like a trapped animal.

"Go, Stacy. She needs me."

Stacy nodded, but Jason paid no attention. He ran into the room and swung his chain in a wide arc above him, preparing to take out as many of Melissa's attackers as he could with one blow.

He reached them, and the weighted end of the eight feet of chain he let loose smashed across them like a hammer, taking out four of them in a neat row.

He saw Nick running towards them. He saw Blitz engaged with two men to his left - and then he saw Melissa look over at Nick. He saw in her eyes that she was beyond recognizing the difference between enemy and friend.

8

Melissa leaped at him with a scream filled with more rage than he had ever heard her muster. She barreled over two men. Nick stopped in his tracks, unsure of what to do, but Melissa did not share his hesitation. She hit him with the force of an enraged bull.

The two of them hit the ground hard and slid a good five or six feet on the concrete floor. Melissa dropped her staff and just started punching.

"Melissa, no!" Jason screamed, but she didn't seem to hear him.

He swung his weapon in a wide circle, taking out three more of his attackers. With that he broke off towards his friends. He would have to trust Blitz to protect them and Stacy to take out anyone who made a run for the door.

If he didn't do something, Melissa was going to kill their friend.

Jason jumped over two fallen cultists and a smashed table, just making it to Melissa in time to grab a raised fist about to crash down into Nick's already battered face.

"Melissa, stop it! What's wrong with you?!" he screamed.

She paid him no mind, and she was strong. She pulled her hand away from him with ease and hit Nick again for what must have been the fourteenth or fifteenth time. Nick himself was just lying there, trying to defend himself but unwilling and unable to fight back. The shock of what was happening partnered with the blunt force trauma she was inflicting had left him nearly paralyzed.

Jason decided to try another tactic. Melissa was strong, but he was stronger. He wrapped his large arms around her and gripped her in an iron-clad bear hug.

She screamed and fought against him, her eyes still locked on Nick and her legs gripping him as Jason tried to lift her off her former friend and current victim.

He finally pulled her off of him, and held her above the ground as she struggled and kicked.

Nick managed to push himself away from them a couple of inches and then just stopped. His eyes closed, and his head hit the concrete. Melissa had beaten him into unconsciousness.

Jason shook her and spoke softly but sternly into her ear.

"Melissa, it's me. It's Jason. You hurt Nick, Melissa. You hurt our friend."

With that, Melissa's struggling seemed to weaken a bit. Her cries began to sound more pitiful than angry.

"I'm not going to hurt you, Melissa. No one's going to hurt you. I promise."

That stopped her. She went limp in his arms and began to cry. He sat down on the floor, still holding her. She held him back.

"I'm so sorry, Jason. I'm so sorry. It's like I was back there. It's like he was hurting me again and I just…couldn't stop myself."

"Who was hurting you?" he asked her. She didn't answer. She just shook her head and buried her face in his shoulder. He picked her up and looked around. The room was empty except for a number of bruised and beaten cultists who no longer posed a threat to anyone. Blitz must have chased the others out.

"It's time to get the hell out of here."

2

"The Hero," they were now calling him, some papers having dropped the "masked" portion now that he was being viewed as a savior rather than a menace. It was unusual for the media to give such a generalized name, but somehow it had stuck, and now the tales of the dark-garbed, dark-masked, sword-wielding defender were appearing almost daily in side stories on the nightly news, articles in the newspapers, and in the mouths of people everywhere. He was, for some reason, becoming especially popular with the lower class, low-income families, perhaps because of his reported saving of a poor black woman's child from the burning house those many months ago.

Of course, there were many who looked at it all with intense skepticism. There really couldn't be such a thing as a man who defended the weak, fought off evil, and put himself in jeopardy for the lives of others so often, could there? That was comic book stuff. But despite all of the raised brows and the chuckles of disbelief, the reports kept coming. Thomas Cross was keeping track. The so-called Hero was becoming a fascination of his.

He was first seen in Atlanta, by a black woman by the name of Ellen May and her son, James May. Next, two teenagers were found mutilated in a back alley-way by what forensics found to be a curved blade. Not but a day later, an elderly couple reported to police that they had been harassed by a large group of thugs, only to be saved by a man wearing a mask. This event took place right next door to the scene of the previous night's murder.

About a week later, police received reports of a scuffle outside of the RavenCorp building involving an unidentified woman and a masked man. Witness descriptions matched the elderly couple's previous sketch perfectly. Two weeks later, the suspect was reported by Raven's security force to have played a part in a deadly confrontation which left Sergeant William Cross, Thomas's uncle, dead. Stacy Cross, his daughter and Tom's cousin, also reportedly at the scene that night, was still missing.

Then the suspect disappeared from Atlanta entirely. The masked stranger seemed to pop out of the limelight just as quickly as he had appeared.

However, the murders that had accompanied him continued. A shooting range in Alabama was broken into in late February, it's eight patrons slaughtered with a curved blade. A girl was found decapitated alongside the interstate on the way to Mississippi. Strangest of all, a train had been derailed near Jackson, killing fourteen people. The train engineer's official statement was that the train had come off the tracks after he had "plowed over a metal monster with fingers like swords."

Now, in early June, Detective Tom Cross was investigating a series of brutal slayings in New Orleans. The common factor in all of these cases: the murder weapon had been determined to be a curved blade. Cross was convinced that he had a serial killer on the loose and that the murderer he now searched for and the mysterious "Hero" who had recently re-appeared in New Orleans were one and the same.

"Detective Cross, come take a look at this," came the voice of a young police officer from behind where Tom Cross was standing.

Thomas had been staring at a two-foot-long gouge in the wooden wall above the dead fisherman's body. The mark had probably been made by the same blade that had severed the dead man's head, which now lay covered by a small tarp at Cross's feet. Cross wondered if the fatal wound and the mark in the wall had been made simultaneously in one swipe, since the man seemed to have died while standing in front of this very wall.

He now turned and walked over to where the young officer was crouched. As he approached, he got a good look at the thing in the dirt that the officer was staring at. A large footprint was imprinted there, but it was not like any footprint Cross had ever seen.

"What the hell?"

"It looks like an overgrown bird print, sir. My mother kept chickens back on the farm when I was a kid, and I know chicken tracks when I seen them," the patrolman commented.

"So you're saying this man was killed by an overgrown poultry product?" Cross said, not even a hint of amusement in his voice.

"N...no, sir. I just mean...it looks like a print a bird would make - something with talons. See them?"

Cross nodded. The print did make him think of a predatory bird. He had to admit he had no idea where a print like this could have come from.

"Make a mold of it - we'll check it out later." Cross said, turning back to the spot in the fisherman's shack where the body was just being covered.

This scene matched the killer's M.O. perfectly - slashes on the surroundings, wounds made with a curved blade, murder committed with simultaneous surgical precision and incredible savagery.

Cross wanted into the FBI so badly that he would almost sell his mother for it, and finding a killer of this caliber would look damn good on his record. This was the very reason he had traveled so far from his home precinct to assist in this case - that and he wanted to check up on his cousin. Tracking Stacy down hadn't been that difficult. She had applied for a job at a diner outside of town several months ago. Her ID had pinged on a search Tom had set up after her father's death.

He would check up on Stacy soon enough. He had no reason to suspect she was in danger after sending a NOPD officer into the diner to covertly check up on her. His main priority was to follow the case of the Hero and the Demon. Assuming, as Thomas thought, they weren't possibly one and the same.

"Wake up."

Nick slowly opened his eyes, trying to focus on the face looming above him.

"Look, Blitz, the patient's awake," Stacy said, smiling while she cradled Nick's head on her lap.

Nick felt a wet tongue on the side of his face.

"Aaugh!" Nick exclaimed, which was quickly followed by "Ow."

"Yeah, I bet you hurt. I was afraid Melissa turned your face into hamburger."

Nick sat up slowly. His head felt like a busted watermelon.

"Where is she? What happened?"

Stacy's smile told him everything was alright, and that eased his fears.

"She's upstairs with Jason. He's been trying to calm her down since we got home. She had some kind of…breakdown."

Nick nodded, rubbing his bruised cheekbone.

"I noticed."

Stacy nodded back and then continued.

"Jason got Melissa to the car and then went back for you. I called the cops after we mopped up the rest of the cultists, for whatever good it'll do. We were well out of there by the time they showed up. I also called an ambulance for the survivor. He was in pretty bad shape."

"The survivor?" Nick asked.

"There was only one," Stacy noted sadly.

Nick sighed. So their daring raid was only partially successful.

"At least we got one out," he said.

"Yeah, and maybe put a bunch of psychos in jail. With Raven gone, we're all hoping the police can actually do their jobs now."

Nick nodded, though he would have traded the lives of those innocent people for the "justice" brought against their captors any day.

The two of them heard a door close upstairs, followed by footsteps descending towards the living room.

Melissa entered first. She looked up and saw Nick and then immediately averted her eyes. She was ashamed to look at him, it seemed

Jason followed her. He also looked at Nick, though his eyes widened instead of looking away.

"Damned if you aren't invincible, kid. Why your brain isn't sticking out of your ears after that beating is beyond me," he said.

"See? I told you," Stacy said cheerfully, as if she had no doubt that Nick would be fine.

Melissa walked around the corner of the couch. To Nick's pleasant surprise, she moved around Stacy and sat right next to him.

She wrapped him in a big hug. He could feel her cheek, wet from recent tears, against his.

"I'm so sorry, Nick," she whispered to him.

Nick hugged her back and gently shook his head.

"I know you didn't mean it. Besides, now you can actually say you've beaten me in a fight for once."

14

"Asshole," Melissa said, though when she pulled away, Nick could see she was grinning ear to ear, obviously relieved at his forgiveness.

"But now," Nick said, sitting back. "you need to tell us what exactly happened. What made you lose control like that?"

Stacy and Jason watched her closely as she crossed her arms in front of her and sat back on the couch. She seemed to stare off into somewhere only she could see.

"Memories," she said. "Memories are what happened back there."

Nick looked at Jason, but he only shrugged. Melissa hadn't shared much about her past since they had known her. They had never thought it necessary to ask. Now, it seemed that things had changed.

"I know I've never told you guys much about who I was or what happened to me before RavenCorp. I never really wanted to think about it myself, honestly. There are a lot of things I kind of…blocked out over the years. I guess it's all still in me."

She looked at them.

"And I guess after sticking by me for so long, you all deserve the truth."

Nick flashed back to his own similar "coming clean" moment not so long ago, and understood how she felt.

Melissa rubbed her hands together slowly, as if preparing herself for something difficult, and then went on.

"I think I've told you that my mother died when I was young. Very young. Twelve years old, actually. Seems like forever ago - but I remember her. She was the world to me - my best friend and my protector. The only good thing I ever had."

Nick looked at Stacy and Jason, who both had effectively lost their mothers as well. Nick, himself, did not remember his.

"After she was gone, it was just me and my dad. I was never really close to him. I don't think he was capable of being close to anyone but Mom, but when she died he seemed to get worse. A lot worse. He started drinking. He ignored me half the time and spent the other half yelling at me and blaming me for everything he could think of. I was an only child, so there was no one else in the house for him to take his frustration out on. Eventually he started…beating me as well," she said. Her face was angry, but her eyes were sad. Nick wanted to hold her. They all did. But for now he knew the best thing was to listen.

"But that wasn't the worst of it," she continued. "Oh no."

She seemed to gather herself for what came next, and Nick dreaded what could be worse than a father who beat her.

"He had a brother. My uncle David. I never saw him while my mom was around, but after she was gone, David was one of the only people to talk to my father and I think I know why he came into the picture when it was just me and Dad. He was interested in me."

Nick could see Jason out of the corner of his eye gripping the arm of his chair in anger. He couldn't blame him one bit.

"David started asking if I could come over. My dad didn't care what happened to me at that point, so he would take me over there, drop me off, and then leave for the afternoon - probably to get wasted in a bar somewhere. The first time I came over, David acted really nice at first, but not a good kind of nice. David was nice like a snake. He gave me ice cream, and I think there was something in it. It made me sleepy. Still awake, but kind of…out of it, and then he slipped a black bag over my head and carried me downstairs."

Stacy put a hand over her mouth. None of them were sure if they wanted to hear any more but knew that, for Melissa's sake, they had to.

"I heard voices when we got down there. I was so scared because I realized that there were other people in the house besides me and David. None of those voices sounded nice. Not even snake-nice, like David. They just sounded…hungry."

Melissa leaned forward. Her eyes were distant. It was as if she had opened the floodgates of memory and now couldn't stop herself.

"I felt him tie me up to a wall. Chains and handcuffs, the whole nine yards. I felt him take my clothes off. He took the bag off of my head, and I saw them. I was too drugged to know how many, but the whole room was full of them. People in robes, just like the crackpots we took out earlier. There were things drawn on the walls. Vile, foreign things and writing I didn't understand. I saw David, and he was dressed just like them. No…that's not true. He had a suit on under his robe. A really expensive suit, because he was the leader. He was holding a knife. I tried to scream, but someone stuffed a gag in my mouth, and then they…did things to me."

Melissa's face twisted into a mask of pain and fear. The flood had released too much. She was reliving what had happened to her, and not even the tough-as-nails warrior they all knew could handle it all.

Stacy wrapped her arms around her and laid her head on Melissa's shoulder. Nick put an arm around her other shoulder and smoothed her hair out of her face while she wept.

Jason didn't move. All he did was sit there and hold onto his chair as if it were taking all he had to keep himself from attacking something.

Finally, she calmed down. She nodded to Nick and Stacy and scooted away from them. She then placed her hands around the collar of her shirt and pulled it down.

They all saw. Her chest was criss-crossed with deep scars. Old scars.

Jason's mouth fell open, but he still could not say a word.

"That went on for about a year and a half," she said, having regained control of herself. "About once a month, David would call, my dad would bring me over there, and it would all happen again. Then one day David just stopped calling. He moved, apparently, and he and his friends probably found some other young girl to torment.

"You didn't tell your dad while it was happening?" Stacy asked.

"Of course I did," Melissa answered. "and he told me I was a liar. He couldn't believe that his brother was a sadistic wack-job, but he was more than happy to believe that his daughter was a lying whore. I think that's what…flipped the switch for me."

The anger and resolve were back in her face. Nick hoped that meant the worst was passed.

"After David was gone and I was left with my pain and confusion and anger, I started turning that anger towards my father. He still beat me. I would have taken those beatings any day over what David did, but now when my father hit me I started silently saying to myself, 'Soon it will be the last time.'"

"I didn't run away then like most girls would have. No, I wanted to hurt someone back, and all I had was my dad. So I started training myself. I started working out every day and spending time beating on the heavy bag in the garage when my father was passed out."

Now Melissa started actually smiling.

17

"And I discovered…I was good at it. Really good. I took to violence like a fish takes to water. It was almost like I was possessed by something. Or I was…tapping in to something that had always been there. It was just so easy. I would watch Kung Fu movies and then I would act out what I saw those men do, and more often than not I found that I could move just like they did. Well sure, it was awkward at first, but eventually…it wasn't any more. Eventually I was a pro."

They all noted the strange satisfaction in her eyes. The same kind of satisfaction a professional basketball player probably feels as he remembers the first time he made a slam dunk during a home game.

"One day I was working on the heavy bag, and I hit it so hard that the chain snapped and it flew across the room. That's when I decided that it was time. I marched into my dad's den without any kind of plan. I stood over him in his chair and I told him to get the fuck up."

"He looked at me like I had just slapped him in the face. So he got up, called me a disrespectful bitch, and then took a swing at me."

She sighed and sat back against the couch, still smiling.

"I blocked it. I think that shocked him even worse than what came next. After he tried to hit me, I hit him back. I slugged him square in the face and he went tumbling backwards over his chair. I wasn't about to stop there. I had spent too much time preparing for it. So I walked around the chair, pulled him up off the ground - now keep in mind this was a two-hundred-and-fifty-pound man and I was a teenage girl just on the edge of sixteen - and punched him again. I let him fall and then I started kicking him and punching him and just…letting all of that hurt and anger go all over him. I think…I think I nearly killed him, to tell you the truth. I didn't take the time to find out. When he was broken and bleeding enough to suit me, I just walked out the door. Well…I took his wallet, but then I walked out the door. I didn't stop walking for a long time."

With that, she seemed satisfied. The others looked at her in bewilderment and anticipation, but Melissa herself seemed pleased. The cat had finally been let out of the bag. Her past was no longer an unspoken, un-confronted relic locked away in some closet in her mind. Now it was out, and she seemed to feel better for it.

"Well, then what happened?" Stacy finally said, breaking the silence.

Melissa seemed a little surprised by the question. In fact, she seemed surprised that anyone else was in the room at all.

"Oh. Well...then I started trying to find my way in the world. All I really knew how to do was fight, so that's what I did. I got into fights at nearly every bar in eastern Alabama. I always won. Eventually that got me noticed, and I started getting invited to participate in freestyle fighting competitions. Totally underground stuff."

"Well, I beat the pants off of everyone who went against me. I won every title there was to win, and that's when Raven found me. You all know what happened after that."

Nick put his face in his hands. He truly didn't know what to say.

Melissa, on the other hand, seemed to be completely at ease. All of the pain and anger and shame that had been on her face during her long tale was now totally gone, replaced by a kind of calm serenity.

She stood up and clapped her hands together.

"So, who wants coffee?"

3

Nick sat on the back porch railing, staring out over the lake. Jason had joined him a few moments ago and was leaning silently against the wall, also looking out over the water, his dark glasses doing little to hide his somber expression.

"What do we do about this?" Nick asked.

Jason shook his head.

"Not a damn thing, Nick. There's not a damn thing we can do."

Nick sighed. All he could think about were those scars covering Melissa's chest and the kind of person her uncle must have been to leave them.

"She suffered so much, and she never told us any of it over the nine months we've been with her."

"Would you?" Jason asked.

Nick thought about it and shrugged.

"Probably not. You know I kept things from the rest of you for a long time. Melissa more than earned her right to do the same. I just wish I had known. Then I could have…well…."

Nick ran a hand through his dark hair, feeling more helpless than he'd felt in a while.

"I don't know," he finished. The truth was, he knew that there wouldn't have been anything he could have done for Melissa. Her past was hers to bear.

"I will tell you that while I heard her talk about her uncle, and her father, I was more angry then than I'd ever been at Raven," Jason said. "If either of them had been there, I would have murdered them with my bare hands."

Nick nodded. Though he handled anger better than Jason, it was hard to disagree.

"But she's so strong," Nick said, smiling a little. "To be able to just…bounce back like that. To seem so chipper and normal after telling us about a childhood full of abuse…. She's made of tougher stuff than I am."

21

"Tougher stuff than all of us," Jason agreed.

Nick looked up at him. "She needs you, you know that?"

Jason shifted uncomfortably, but Nick went on.

"She needs you more than the rest of us because she trusts you more. You're like her…I don't know…her safe spot."

Jason looked down at his feet.

"The last thing I am right now, Nick, is safe."

Nick couldn't argue. Jason's vendetta wasn't healthy for any of them to be around. But then neither was Nick's demon stalker, and no one had complained about The Whisper since their first encounter - which had also been their last encounter, for which Nick thanked the heavens.

"Still," Nick said. "she needs you - and I think you need her."

Jason raised his eyebrows.

"The pot calls the kettle black."

Nick looked confused for a moment but then realized what Jason was trying to say.

"Stacy," Nick said.

Jason nodded.

"You know I can't, Jason. You have to understand that. Things could…go wrong with me at any time. I could get killed on the street. The Whisper could decide to stop playing around and actually murder me. Or my past could catch up to me in ways I can't even foresee. Stacy doesn't deserve that."

"Isn't that for her to say?" Jason disagreed.

Nick just shook his head.

"This isn't just about me, Jason. Or Stacy."

Jason shrugged. "Fair enough. I was just saying."

Nick didn't reply and looked back out over the water.

"But maybe you're right," Jason said. "about Melissa needing me. I have to get her mind off of things."

Nick looked back at Jason and smiled.

"Good."

"So let's see, what does Melissa like to do?" Jason asked himself out loud.

"Hit things…scream at things…think about hitting and screaming at things…drive her motorcycle like a maniac…and drink like a sailor."

Nick chuckled at Jason's inventory of Melissa's interests.

"Take her to a bar, then," Nick said.

Jason shrugged and nodded.

22

"That works. If she drinks enough, she may end up doing all the rest of those things anyway."

A few hours later, Melissa was well on her way to fulfilling Jason's prediction.

She slammed her empty bottle down on the counter.

"Time for round six," she said.

"Dear lord," Jason muttered, lightly shaking his head in amazement.

"What?" Melissa looked over at him.

"You realize it's only been thirty minutes since we got here. You know what? Nevermind," Jason replied. "Bartender? Let's have another round over here."

"Damn straight," Melissa added.

The establishment was a large country-style bar and dance hall. Southern rock blared over speakers and middle-aged Patsy Clines and Johnny Cashes strutted their stuff and flirted, and often stumbled drunkenly, on the dance floor behind them.

After Melissa's sixth beer and Jason's second were delivered to them, Melissa raised her bottle in a salute.

"Cheers, mate. And thanks," she said to Jason.

"Don't mention it. This is doing us both some good."

"Yeah, it's good to get away from Emo Boy and Princess Happy-Pants every once in a while, just the two of us," she said.

Jason smiled. "Well then, we should do this more often."

Melissa nodded eagerly.

Jason could still see a distance in her eyes. Some part of her was still far away. Had been all evening.

"You know, I took you here to get you away from your problems. But from the look of you, you brought some of them with us," he told her.

She kept a slight smile on her face, but her shoulders slumped a bit.

"You always could read me like a book," she said.

"Or a magazine," he said. "Like Guns and Ammo."

That got her laughing again. She turned to him, and he was pleased to see a twinkle in her eye.

"Jason," she said. "if I were to ask you to go somewhere with me, take a road trip for a few days, would you?"

Jason didn't hesitate.

"Of course I would."

She smiled.

"Good. I'm…thinking about doing something. Putting a part of the past behind me. I've been avoiding it for years…allowing myself to believe I didn't have to do it…but now, after what happened…I think I do."

"You want me to help you find David?" Jason asked, eager to track down the son of a bitch that hurt her.

"No," she shook her head. "my father."

He sat back in his chair.

"Alright. Just us?"

"Just us," she replied, smiling. "We'll let Blitz babysit the kids while we're away."

He smiled. "Sounds about right."

The two of them turned their attention back to their beers and listened to some country warbler belt out a song about how his wife left him for a man with a better pickup truck. They were both left wondering why they had not chosen a better bar.

A metallic clank rang out behind them as Melissa drained the last of beer number six. Jason turned to look.

"Holy shit," he said slowly.

Melissa removed the bottle from her lips and looked into the mirror behind the bar just in time to see a body flying towards them.

Melissa and Jason dove apart as a three-hundred-pound man came crashing into and over the bar between them, smashing into the mirror and busting it into a million pieces.

She spun towards the direction the living projectile had come from, and the blood nearly froze in her veins.

"Holy shit is right."

Hanging by one arm like a monkey from a thick wooden rafter was The Whisper. His glowing purple eyes were fixed on them, and his sickening grin made him look pleased at what he had done. His feet were planted on the wall, and the long bladed fingers of his other arm drug on the floor, leaving trails of the man's blood across the wooden tile.

"Creep knows how to make an entrance," she said.

The bar patrons were now screaming in terror, piling towards the exits. The bar staff followed, and Jason and Melissa could see one or two of them frantically calling 911 on their cell phones. Thankfully, The Whisper seemed to be letting them go. His attention was fixed on Jason and Melissa, and his eyes seemed to tell them that the next move was theirs.

"What do we do?" Jason asked her.

"What we do best," she answered, a sly smile starting to cross her face.

Now Jason was concerned.

"Are you insane!? He beat the crap out of both of us last time! And you've had six beers!"

"Just sharpened my focus," she said.

Jason sighed and flicked his wrist, letting his chain drop from his sleeve in its usual hiding spot.

Melissa saw Jason's weapon and started grinning.

"Now let's show Metal-Head we know how to party," she said and took off running toward The Whisper.

The demon's smile widened, and he jumped down off the wall to meet her charge.

Half way across the room, Melissa picked up a chair and flung it at him.

The Whisper sliced through the chair like a piñata. The chair, however, had only been a distraction. Melissa slammed into him with a shoulder charge.

The demon barely budged, and Melissa bounced off and stumbled to the ground.

"Well, shit," she said.

"Didn't you learn last time not to throw yourself at the guy?" Jason yelled.

Melissa rolled backwards just in time to avoid getting cut up with the floorboards beneath her, now shredded like newspaper.

"You never know until you try," she answered him. "Twice."

Jason joined her, and roared as he swung at The Whisper's feet. Jason, unlike Melissa, had learned from last time.

His chain, up until now hidden and wrapped around his forearm beneath his sleeve, wrapped around the demon's taloned foot. Melissa tried to take advantage of the distraction by throwing roundhouse kicks at the monster's grinning head.

The Whisper surprised them both by spinning his entire body horizontally through the air, unwinding himself from Jason's chain while slashing at Melissa.

"Whoa!" she said, double-stepping away from the attack.

Jason grimaced and desperately tried to think of a way to effectively attack their strange and dangerous assailant.

The Whisper did not stop moving. He threw himself towards Jason, slashing him painfully across both arms before kneeing him in the stomach. Sensing Melissa attack from behind, the demon kicked out towards the back, catching her in the forehead.

Melissa's head snapped back, and she flew back into a table, smashing it in half.

"Are you ok!?" Jason screamed, desperately trying to scramble away from The Whisper.

Melissa sat up, rubbing her head.

"Sort of," was her reply.

Jason stayed low, shoving tables and chairs in between himself and the monster as The Whisper pursued.

"Melissa! I've got an idea! I'm going to give you an opening, and when I do, I want you to hit him as hard as you can, okay?" he screamed across the room.

"Don't have to ask me twice," she answered, getting back to her feet.

Jason maneuvered back towards the bar, and when he and The Whisper were in front of it, he stood back up. The Whisper came slashing towards him. Jason waited.

When the demon was right in front of him, Jason looped his chain around one of The Whisper's arms, and then jumped up onto the counter. He ran across the counter top. The Whisper swiped at him with his other arm, just as Jason had planned.

He wrapped the other end of his chain around the other arm and then jumped up and over The Whisper. The demon screamed, and Jason pulled with all his might, pinning both of The Whisper's arms behind him. He then yanked them around, facing away from the bar and towards Melissa. He prayed she would be there in time to spare him from being skewered by those far-too-close blades.

And there she was. Within seconds, Melissa crashed into The Whisper's face with a flying kick. Jason ducked and let go of the chain, letting the demon fly up and over the bar, smashing into the same wall he had flung that poor man earlier.

"Whoo yeah!" Melissa yelled triumphantly.

Jason grabbed her arm.

"Now let's get the hell out of here."

"What about your…" she said, trying to look around the bar.

"I'll get another one," he replied. "Now let's go!"

They ran out of the bar as fast as their legs could carry them. Melissa jumped onto her motorcycle, revving it up as Jason got on behind her. Then they were moving, pulling out of the parking lot and onto the two-lane highway.

Jason looked behind them, and as they were rounding the corner away from the bar, he saw The Whisper stroll out the door and watch them go, still wearing that infernal grin.

"Hah!" Melissa screamed. "We kicked his metal ass!"

"Don't be so cocky. All we did was buy ourselves time to escape," he said.

"Fine, whatever," she replied. "Killjoy."

Jason peeked behind them again, but didn't see anything.

"Why do you think he came after us tonight? I thought all he cared about was Nick?" Jason spoke loudly into her ear above the roar of the engine and the whipping of the wind as Melissa sped down the road.

"Nick said he thought the thing might want to mess with us. Just for…I don't know…fun," she said.

"That thing has a sick idea of fun," Jason replied.

He looked behind them again. At first, all he saw were the headlights of cars on the road behind them. Then he caught a glint of metal among the tree tops in the corner of his eye.

"Oh no. Speed up! Now!"

Melissa did, and as the engine of her small Harley roared, The Whisper came diving out of the trees from the woods on their right. He hit the pavement just inches behind them. Jason was very aware of how close he had come to being cleaved in half.

"How the hell did he catch up with us?" Melissa yelled, keeping her eyes focused on the road.

Jason watched the monster quickly rise from the crater it had left in the pavement. It started running, and in an instant it was suddenly gaining on them.

"Oh. That's how," she said, seeing him in her rearview mirror.

The Whisper's legs and arms pumped inhumanly fast, easily gaining on the motorcycle, which Melissa was now pushing to seventy miles an hour. As she wove through traffic, The Whisper wove with her. Thicker than the slim motorcycle, the monster shoved cars out of the way like a linebacker, sending a sedan and a small jeep careening into the guardrail.

"Shit!" Jason exclaimed, suddenly panicked. "Shit, shit, shit, shit."

He frantically tried to think of something he could do to get the creature off of their tail. If it caught up to them, Jason would be the first to be cut to ribbons.

He suddenly thought of the side bags on the back of Melissa's bike. He tore one of them open and started rifling through its contents, looking for something - anything - that might help them.

He pulled out a short rubber tie-down cord with a hook on each end. Jason thought for a moment.

Yeah, it just might work.

He twisted himself around. He held the cord above his and Melissa's heads and began swinging it like he would his chain.

"Come on. Come on," he muttered below his breath. He knew he would only get one shot at this.

The Whisper was very close. Just ten feet away, Jason guessed.

Close enough.

Jason let go of the cord, slinging it towards The Whisper. He threw it low, and it wrapped around the legs of their monstrous pursuer.

For an instant, Jason thought he saw an expression of shock replace the grin on The Whisper's face, and then it was tumbling and crashing down the road behind them. He saw the demon smash into a van, sending it careening into another car, which was then hit by a third vehicle.

"Did you do that?" Melissa asked, hearing the collision behind her.

"Yeah," Jason replied. "Oops."

The two of them then heard a frustrated howl echo into the night air far behind them.

They waited almost a minute before saying anything else, so concerned were they that the monster would simply catch right back up.

But he never did. Being thrown into a van was apparently enough to cause The Whisper to hang up his hat for the night.

"So, now will you admit that we beat him?" Melissa asked.

"We got lucky," was his response.

"Potato, potahto," Melissa said, shaking her head. "In my book we're not dead or unconscious, so that means we won."

Jason didn't disagree.

"Just don't tell Nick about this," he said.

"Yeah. Poor kid doesn't need this on his conscience, too," she agreed.

They rode a few more miles before Melissa spoke again.

"So, uh…now that the adrenaline's wearing off…I'm kinda drunk. Do you want to drive us the rest of the way home?"

Jason laughed.

"Gladly."

4

His bones felt on the verge of crumbling. His muscles felt like they were being devoured by fire ants. Every breath was quick and shallow because his ribs had been broken in a dozen different places.

And yet Jacob Raven had never felt more powerful in his life.

He had survived. He had fallen from a height that would have killed a normal man instantly, and yet he lived. He was healing…at an accelerated rate. Something was watching over him. Something favored him, just as he had always known.

He was invincible.

If only he could button up his own shirt.

"Let me help, sir," Francis McElroy said as he took the buttons from Raven's trembling hands. Both of Raven's arms were in casts. One of his legs was still badly broken. His ribs and pelvis were healing, and he would likely walk with a cane for the rest of his life. Kind of ironic, considering Raven had only carried one previously for dramatic effect.

"Thank you, Francis. One day soon I'll be able to do that myself again," Raven said to him.

Ordinarily, Raven's appearance was a bit impish. His light blonde hair was shortly cropped and his facial hair shaped into a groomed goatee. He stood a mere 5'7", a size which did little to mask the effect of power he radiated. Raven was a powerful man and his air of confidence showed it. Now, however, he couldn't help but appear a bit...lessened.

"No problem, sir," McElroy replied, finishing up with the top button, then straightening Raven's collar.

"You're too good to me," Raven told him, thankful to have at least one friend in the world.

"Thanks," McElroy said, seeming genuinely surprised.

"But still…," McElroy continued. "I wish you would trust me more sometimes, sir."

Raven sighed. He knew what this was about.

"And trust him less?" Raven asked.

McElroy backed up a step, suddenly worried that he had offended his boss.

"I just...don't like him, sir. He isn't natural. Well, you know that. I don't think he really has your best interests at heart."

Raven laughed a little.

"I don't disagree."

McElroy looked confused.

"Then why do you still listen to him?"

Raven looked up at Francis, and his eyes turned deadly serious.

"Because the man is pure power. You've only seen a fraction of what he can do. The things I've seen.... He's offering me some of that power, Francis. A power that is my birthright. Wherever or whatever he gets it from wants me to have it, too. And when I can finally take it from him...I won't need to listen to him anymore."

McElroy nodded, looking a little more satisfied.

"Besides," Raven said. "I know that if he ever crosses the line, I have loyal men there to help me stop him."

At this, McElroy straightened his shoulders and smiled.

"My associate serves his purpose for now, Francis. I only ask that you trust my judgment. I'll only use him as long as necessary."

"Yes, sir."

There was a knock on the office door. One of Raven's guards popped his head in.

"They're here, sir."

Raven smiled.

"Good. Let them in."

The man hesitated.

"I have to warn you, sir. They're a little...."

Raven waited, but the man seemed reluctant to continue.

"Well? A little what?"

The man shook his head.

"Never mind, sir. You'll see."

Raven and McElroy shared a concerned look. A few moments later, the door opened, and the two of them began to understand what the guard had been warning them about.

The man who entered the room was a curious figure indeed. He was dressed in an old, brown Victorian jacket, complete with ruffled sleeves. His pants were long, brown slacks and his shoes were dark leather with big, golden buckles.

A long rapier with an ornate swept silver hilt was strapped to his side. His face was worn and rugged, yet regal and handsome despite his age. He wore a long scar from the middle of his forehead to the middle of his cheek, crossing his right eye. His hair was a brilliant shock of white, short and combed forward.

The man bowed gracefully as he reached the center of the room.

"Byron, sir. A pleasure to make your acquaintance," the man said, still bowing.

Raven shared another amused look with McElroy.

"Well hello, Mr. Byron. Thank you for answering my call."

"Just Byron, sir," the man said, standing back to his full height of nearly six feet. "and you're welcome. My associates and I are always in the market for interesting work."

"Good," Raven answered. "And may I see these...associates?"

Byron nodded, and looked back towards the door. Apparently his wordless summons was received, because the door quickly opened.

Two more men and a woman entered the room.

One man was tall - a good several inches above McElroy, which was saying a lot. He was also several inches wider than McElroy, which was saying even more. He was built like a body-builder who had a genetically large frame to begin with. He wore an unassuming tank-top and jeans, with a red bandanna wrapped around his dark hair. A sawed-off shotgun was strapped to a holster around his back.

The woman was medium height - about five-foot-six - but her face made her look just as intimidating as the much larger man. She was Asian, and wore black face paint smeared around her eye sockets. She scowled as she entered, and the lines in her face told Raven that she likely wore that scowl all the time. Her clothes were just as simple as the man's - a black spandex gym outfit. It reminded him of the brown and grey outfits Melissa Moonbeam used to wear. Something that Melissa lacked, however, were the leather bands with long steel spikes wrapped around this woman's wrists and ankles.

But it was the third figure that impressed Raven the most. He was small as well - only about an inch taller than the woman. He wore what looked like a black cloak around a tattered priest's uniform, complete with collar. His hair was long, straggly, and ebony black, and his skin was as pale as moonlight. His eyes were wide and staggeringly blue. A kind of ice blue that's difficult to look at for long. There seemed to be no soul behind them. At his side was the most-wicked looking weapon that Raven had ever seen. It was a whip coiled up beside his belt, and inserted through the leather throughout were small, cruelly sharp razor blades. A spiked barb swayed from the tip.

Raven couldn't even begin to imagine how such a weapon functioned.

"Well," Raven called out. "I'm impressed. I love colorful criminals."

Byron turned to his colleagues, motioning towards the large man first.

"Brick," he said, and the large man nodded.

"Bitch," he then said, motioning towards the woman.

"And Razorpriest," he finished with the small man with the whip.

"Of course," Raven said, amused by the ironically obvious names.

Byron turned back to Raven, and the four of them seemed to await instruction.

"And now, sir, it is time to tell us exactly who this 'interesting quarries' you promised us are."

Raven sat back in his chair, trying to pretend he was not in serious pain.

"All in due time, my good man. First, I need a demonstration. To see if you're as good as everyone says you are."

McElroy muttered something into his mouthpiece, and in a few short moments, the doors to the office opened again and six of Raven's men entered in full riot gear, armed with stun batons. They surrounded Byron's crew.

Byron didn't look in the least bit surprised.

"Kill them," Raven ordered, though it was uncertain exactly who was meant to kill whom.

His men moved first, charging at the strange "guests".

The attack did not last long.

Byron unsheathed his rapier. He sidestepped towards the three men closest to him and slashed in an elegant figure-eight. All three of the men fell to the ground clutching bleeding throats.

The woman screamed savagely and threw herself at one of Raven's guards. Her knee hit his facemask and smashed it like plastic. Shards of it dug into the man's face, and he fell back, jerking and spasming as he died.

Brick, the large man, only moved his arm, grabbing his shotgun, twirling it twice in his fingers, and then pulling the trigger. The weapon emitted a deafening roar and opened a large hole in the chest of the man to Brick's left.

Razorpriest's whip seemed to spring to life like a living thing. It uncurled from his side, and his wrist twitched just enough to send its barbed end slicing through a man's facemask and into his eyes.

After Raven's ears stopped ringing from Brick's shotgun blast, he could hear the screams of Razorpriest's victim as he writhed on the floor, clutching his face. Razorpriest himself stared down at the man, his head cocked slightly in curiosity.

To the surprise of all, the injured man rose off of the ground - first to his feet, and then several feet into the air. His screams halted suddenly, and he began clawing at his throat instead of his face.

Razorpriest and Bitch backed away from the man in alarm.

"What trickery is this?" Byron asked.

Raven smiled. He had an idea.

Materializing from the shadows in the corner of his office stepped The Dark Man. His eyes, currently a luminous silver, peered out from beneath his hood.

His hand was outstretched in front of him - his fingers open like a claw. He suddenly and violently closed those fingers. The unfortunate soul suspended in air stopped struggling instantly, his arms and neck going limp. The Dark Man then thrust his arm to his side, and the man sailed across the room, smashing into the wall before sliding to the floor and lying very still.

"Witchcraft," Bitch muttered angrily. She looked as though she was ready to attack.

Byron held his arm out in front of her.

"This one's too powerful for you, child."

The Dark Man stepped forward, hardly casting a glance towards the bounty hunters.

"You'd do best to remember that. All of you," he said as he passed them, making his way to Raven's side.

After The Dark Man took his place beside him, Raven chuckled and turned his attention back to Byron.

"I'm sorry, Byron. My associate here didn't mean to steal your thunder."

Byron seemed tense, but relatively calm considering the circumstances.

"Never mind," he said. "Just tell us what the job is."

"Oh, I've got a good one for you…" Raven said.

Jason, Melissa and their friends were about to gain several deadly new playmates.

5

"Stacy, phone!" Melissa called from the living room.

"We have a phone?" Stacy exclaimed, putting down her newspaper and getting up to answer her.

It was a day after Melissa's breakdown and everyone was on pins and needles except for Melissa. Stacy didn't even know what to say to her. She had plenty of father issues herself. Hell, she had ended up killing hers - but she had never gone through the kind of physical abuse Melissa had. What could you say to someone whose life you could only barely relate to?

"Hello?" Stacy said, picking up the receiver from Melissa's lazily outstretched hand.

"Stacy," said the voice on the other end. "its Thomas. How are you?"

For a moment Stacy couldn't breathe. They weren't supposed to find her. Her family wasn't supposed to ever...

"Relax, Stacy, I'm not calling to lecture you about running off like that. I just want to make sure you're ok."

She felt a bit relieved, but then realized how Thomas had tracked her down. Thomas Cross was an APD detective.

"Tom.... Dad got mixed up with Raven and I just...."

"It's okay," he said reassuringly. "Raven cooperated fully. Your father died in the line of duty - but the way it happened, and with your mother the way she is, I don't blame you for running."

Raven. Raven must have fabricated a story about her father's death.

"I.... Thanks, Tom. I'm fine now, really. I just needed to kind of...start over someplace else."

"I get it. I do. Don't you worry. We'll catch the guy that caused all of this."

"The guy?" she said, surprised.

"That Masked Hero freak. I know your dad was tracking him. I know he was in the warehouse that night. He caused the accident that killed your father. Don't worry. We'll catch him."

Now Stacy really couldn't breathe.

The five of them sat at the table the following evening and stared at each other. Thomas Cross seemed to be studying each of them in turn, and not a one of them was blind to it.

Finally, his eyes rested on Nick. At first, he simply kept that calm smile and peaceful look in his eyes as he had been, but then a spark of something seemed to ignite in his eyes, his brow furrowed, and his smile widened.

"Nick, isn't it?" he asked.

"Yes, that's right." Nick replied. Stacy had invited her cousin over for dinner after his call. In hindsight, she realized it was a mistake, but she did want her surviving family to know she was okay. She had no intention of talking to her mother again, not after the way she worshiped a man Stacy had murdered. Thomas was going to have to do.

"And what is your last name, Nick?"

All three of Nick's friends gritted their teeth as Tom asked this question. They all realized that Thomas was suspicious of the people his cousin had run off with, and if Nick told him that he really didn't know his last name, it would only raise more suspicion.

"I..." Nick started.

"Moonbeam." Melissa finished for him. "He's my brother."

Tom's gaze shifted over to her now, and a sly expression spread across his face. He had made his suspicions and his disbelief quite clear ever since he had entered the building, and Melissa was already forming an acute dislike for the fellow.

"Really? Too bad I don't see the resemblance." Tom said to them.

"Half brother, actually. Illegitimate. My dad had an affair and...well, it's too painful to get into. But I still consider good old Nick there my flesh and blood," Melissa added to the lie, slapping Nick roughly on the back. Tom studied her for an instant more and then nodded. Nick and the others were relieved at Melissa's quick and easy lie.

"C'mon, Tom, let's leave the interrogation till later and focus on eating now. Jason and I cooked spaghetti for five, and now it looks like we're going to end up feeding most of it to Blitz, so let's just eat, okay?" Stacy pleaded with him.

"I'm not interrogating anyone, Stacy. I'm just trying to get to know your friends, here." Tom now shifted his gaze to Jason. "How about you, Mr. Dredd? What do you do?"

"I'm a part-time cook at the diner that Melissa and Stacy work at. But, as Stacy probably told you, the three of us are all looking for a better job right now. We don't exactly enjoy the whole 'truck-stop atmosphere', or the management, for that matter." Jason, who had actually taken his shades off for once, told Cross.

Nick, who had been shoveling spaghetti into his mouth since they had sat down, now picked out a huge meatball and tossed it to his left. The German Shepherd under the table stuck his face out to snatch the flying snack and then retreated to his hiding place to enjoy his meal. This was the fifth such meatball he had been given this evening. Nick returned his attention towards his food and soon finished off the rest of his dinner.

"Never could understand how the boy cold eat that much and still stay so thin," Melissa murmured, shaking her head in exasperation. Nick looked up at her with a big sloppy grin before wiping the spaghetti sauce off of his lips, and then washing it down with a big gulp of water.

Tom laughed. The others were relieved to see that the man had let his guard down for a moment, but that relief soon fled as the detective asked his next question.

"Where are you from, Nick? I have the strangest feeling that I recognize you from somewhere."

Nick looked up at him with wide eyes. "I'm from south of Atlanta. Same as Stacy."

Tom nodded. "South of Atlanta," he echoed.

"That's right. I don't believe I've ever met you before, though. I haven't exactly gotten around to a lot of places during my short, uneventful lifetime." Nick smiled.

Melissa and Jason almost choked on their spaghetti, both greatly amused at the irony of their friend's statement.

"Hmm." Tom looked down at his plate, as if in thought. "So you and Melissa grew up in different states?"

Nick silently cursed himself, threw a glance at Melissa, and nodded.

"Yeah. Like she said, I wasn't exactly the pride of the family. My dad sent me to live with some relatives."

Thomas nodded again, mercifully dropping the subject.

After a few moments, he asked a question directed at all of them. "So what do you all think of this 'Hero' business that's been flying around the papers."

Melissa, Jason, and Stacy almost choked again, but this time not out of amusement. Surprisingly, it was Nick who answered first.

"Well, if you ask me, I think that the media is blowing it all way out of proportion. So what if someone wants to help out some people? Since when is that such a big deal? Why should everyone be surprised at that?"

"It's not so surprising for someone to help others, Mister...Nick...but what is surprising, and I think alarming, is that this particular person goes gallivanting about wearing a mask and carrying a sword. Does that not strike you as somewhat funny?" Tom replied calmly, keeping his eyes locked with Nick's.

"Honestly," Nick returned. "yes, it does. But did you ever stop to think that maybe there's a reason for that? The mask: yes, it makes one think he's a shady character, but at the same time, it makes him something of a mystery, an enigma, something to make people think twice before hurting others in the streets of New Orleans, or wherever it is he's been seen, and something to garner respect and admiration from the people he protects. But more importantly, it makes him larger than life, a hero in the eyes of some - someone who can and will fight for those people, someone to give them hope - the hope that there really are still people out there who believe that goodness is worth fighting for. Take away the mask, and he's just a man - but when he wears that piece of black cloth, he stands for something, he stands for their hopes and dreams. That's why they call him The Hero, Detective Cross, because that's what he is to them, and I assure you that's what he means to be." Nick looked around, suddenly regretting that he had said so much. "At least, that's what I think," he finished lamely.

Good man, Jason thought, happy to see his words to Nick so long ago had sunk in.

Tom's brow raised and his eyes widened in feigned surprise. Nick had given him an earful just then.

"You seem to know a lot about it, Nick." Tom said to him.

Nick shook his head. "Not really, sir, but I like to think that I know something about the human condition, that's all."

Tom smiled and eventually nodded and returned his attention to his meal. The rest of the evening was spent in small-talk and relative silence.

"Tom, they're good people," Stacy said defensively as she walked him to the door.

"Okay. I trust you, Stacy," he said, shrugging his shoulders.

"Then why do I get the feeling you don't?" she asked.

Tom cracked a smile. "I just want to look out for you, Stace. Mom and Dad would kill me if I found out you were in bad company and I did nothing about it."

Stacy's aunt and uncle, Tom's parents, had been the only sane members of the Cross family that Stacy could feel comfortable with. Though she didn't see them often, they were always good to her when she did.

"Tell them I'm fine," she said.

"How long will you be in town?"

"I'm here for a while, it looks like. I'm on loaner to NOPD while we investigate The Masked Hero case."

Great, Stacy thought.

"Tom, it wasn't his fault that night with Dad," she said, knowing full well she was stepping into dangerous territory by talking to him.

"I know. Your dad was hit by friendly fire by Raven's Security forces when the suspect attacked them. He may not have pulled the trigger, but his carelessness and whatever vendetta he has against Raven got your father killed."

Wow. So Raven's lie actually worked out even better than she thought.

"It wasn't that simple. Raven's into some bad things, Tom."

He nodded. "Yeah I know. Everybody in APD and NOPD knows. Whether it's public knowledge or not, he makes our payroll every month, so we have to watch his back."

Stacy sighed. Tom was committed, and she knew her cousin well enough to remember how hard-headed he could be.

"Hey, don't worry your pretty little head over it. I'll catch the bad guys; you just relax and enjoy your time with your friends. If you need me, you know where to find me."

"NOPD," she said. "Right."

"That's right. Just ask for Detective Cross. Got my own desk here and everything," he said smugly.

"Fine," she said, giving him a hug after opening the door. "It is good to see you Tom."

"You too, Stacy. Be good to yourself."

As he left, Stacy felt a stab of guilt rise in her chest. She had seen the way he looked at Nick. If Nick or the others got into trouble because of her....

"Seems like all I can do is let them down," she said, surprising herself

Stacy shook the thought from her mind and closed the door.

6

Nick flipped over the man milliseconds before a blast from a .45 would have opened a hole in Nick's chest. As he flew, he turned around, slashing his opponent across the tender muscle between his neck and his shoulder.

The man screamed, turning around to face Nick, who was now behind him. Before he was fully turned, Nick kicked the pistol from his outstretched hand and then kicked him again in the stomach. The man doubled over. For a moment he seemed to look for his gun, but then Nick's sword hovered before his eyes, and he obviously thought better of it.

"Get out of here. And if I ever see you again, it'll be your arm lying on the ground instead of your gun," Nick said, putting on his usual semi-threatening "Hero" voice.

The man nodded meekly and then took off running down the street. Nick watched him go for a moment before sheathing his sword and turning to the woman the man had been holding up.

"You okay?" he asked her.

She was kneeling on the sidewalk, stroking Blitz. The dog had helped more by calming the woman that he would have aiding in the fight.

The woman looked up at Nick and smiled through her runny mascara.

"Yeah," she sniffed. "Thanks."

"Any time," Nick said before extending a hand to her, helping her to her feet.

She took a closer look at him, and he noticed the concern cross her face.

"Someone take a beating to you?"

Nick realized that his bruises must be visible above his mask. They were fading fast, but Melissa had done a pretty thorough job. Most people would have received a fractured skull from such a beating. He had gotten off lucky.

"Occupational hazard," he said.

"Listen," she said. "I just want you to know…people appreciate what you do. I'm not the only one you've helped. You're important to the people of New Orleans. I'm not sure if you hear that often enough."

Nick smiled. He heard it from time to time, but he was still uncertain how to take such praise.

"Thank you," he said simply. "That means more than you know."

She smiled and nodded.

"Keep at it, Hero. The world needs more of you."

And with that she said her goodbyes and walked away.

Nick took to the shadows and the rooftops and watched her for a while, as he always did, making sure she made it home safely this time. Blitz, in his usual fashion, followed below in the alleys and side streets, playing stray while keeping pace with his friend.

The world needs more of him, she had said.

But Nick knew he was not alone. Melissa, Stacy and Jason were just as heroic as he was. They just didn't stay up until 4 AM wandering the city wearing a mask.

Melissa and Jason would be leaving in a couple of hours. They had told him and Stacy that they were going to go confront Melissa's father. Nick and Stacy both thought it was a great idea and only wished they could be there to help their friend face her demons.

Nick decided he would soon call it a night, but first he wanted to make a stop at the local park. There was something he had been meaning to try.

Sitting beneath the limbs of a huge tree, Nick concentrated. He focused on The Pull. He focused on his memories. He focused on her voice and her eyes.

He was trying to summon her again. He was trying to call the little girl.

She hadn't appeared to him in months. Not since that night when The Whisper had last appeared and he had decided to stay with his friends. Months had passed and he had not heard a word from the only person (if she really was a person) who could give him answers. Answers about who he was, about what The Pull really meant, and where he had come from.

He concentrated - and then opened his eyes.

Nothing.

Nick sighed and propped his head back against the tree. Maybe it was useless. He had only been able to consciously call her once before. Since then she had just appeared whenever it pleased her. And besides, if this little girl was really who Nick hoped she was….

"Hello," came a small voice from directly in front of him.

Nick jumped and his eyes widened.

There she was - plain as day - in the same red and brown dress and same shoes, and with the same crooked teeth, blonde hair and mischievous twinkle in her eye. There was a wisdom in those eyes that betrayed her apparent years and made Nick believe all the more that she was an incarnation of something much greater.

"Hi," Nick said, thoroughly shocked that his summons had actually been answered.

"Looks like you need someone to talk to," she said, swaying back and forth from her heels to the tips of her toes.

"Yeah," he said. "I really do."

She stood there, quietly smiling for a moment before speaking again.

"So talk, silly!"

Nick relaxed a bit, reminding himself that this was a benevolent entity he was talking to. Whoever…whatever she was, she was not out to hurt him.

"You know me, don't you?" he asked.

She giggled.

"Of course. More than anyone."

Nick nodded. "And you could tell me things. About who I am. Where I'm going?"

"Maybe," she answered.

"But you won't," Nick said. "Why?"

"Because life wouldn't mean much if we had all of the answers from the beginning, would it?"

Nick was confused.

"So you want me to keep searching? You don't want me to know who I am?"

"You should trust The Pull, Nick. It will take you where you need to go. But for now…you're with the right people. Stay with your friends. When the time is right and you feel ready, they'll be there beside you, as they should be. As for who you are…."

She smiled knowingly.

"Your past is a lot closer than you think."

45

Nick couldn't help but feel frustrated. Every time the little girl showed up, she always said the same things. Trust The Pull. Listen to yourself.

He was determined to at least get one concrete answer from her this evening.

"Then at least tell me," he said, "what your name is."

She smiled. Nick watched as she looked up at the stars, still rocking on her feet with her arms behind her back, just like a real little girl would. She seemed to be thinking.

"I had a name once," she said. "It was one I gave myself out of a feeling of necessity. You knew it but have forgotten. It doesn't matter now. Just know that I'm someone who can guide you and always has. Also keep in mind that you see me as what you want to see. I'm no more a little girl than you are an ordinary man."

"So I can't even get a clear answer to that," Nick stated in resigned frustration. As for her appearance he had come to the conclusion that this was no run-of-the-mill "little girl" long ago.

Suddenly she turned to the right as if a something had startled her.

"Someone is coming," she said, and Nick saw something in her eyes he didn't like.

Fear.

"I have to go," she said, and then she turned and winked at him, putting him back at ease.

"I won't be far."

She then disappeared. Literally. The little girl in the red and brown dress had blinked out like a light bulb right in front of his eyes.

Nick suddenly became aware of Blitz tensing up beside him. The hackles on the dog's back raised up, and a low growl came from deep in his throat.

Nick stood up and drew his sword. Suddenly, he thought he had an idea at the source of the fear in her eyes.

The Whisper was coming.

Yet it was not The Whisper that emerged from the shadows at the end of the path in front of him. It was a man in a long, black coat.

The man brought his arms before him when he saw Nick and pushed back the hood covering his head.

"Easy now, friend. I mean you no harm," the man said.

Nick relaxed and put his sword away.

"I'm sorry. It's been a weird night," he said apologetically.

"Says the man wearing a mask with a sword strapped to his back."

"Yeah," Nick said. "I get that a lot."

As the man approached, Nick noticed several unusual qualities about the stranger. The first was that he was dressed head-to-toe in black. The second was that he was, in fact, wearing a cloak, not a long coat as he had originally thought. The third was that his eyes were unusually bright. They were a standard blue, but Nick just felt that there was something...off about them.

Nick dismissed him as just another of New Orleans' strange Goth crowd, albeit an older member, as he noticed the man had salt-and-pepper black and grey hair and a matching neatly trimmed beard.

"Who were you talking to?" the man asked.

This put Nick on his guard again. The man had to have been eavesdropping to have overheard his conversation with the little girl.

"No one. Just myself. Like I said...weird night," Nick lied.

The man slowly nodded, stopping his approach just a few feet in front of Nick. His arms were crossed in front of him, and Nick thought he noticed an odd smile on the corner of his lips.

"So...you're this 'Hero' everyone's been talking about?" the man stated, and it was, in fact, more of a statement than a question.

"I'm just a guy. I help where I can, but I'm no different from anyone else."

The man's odd smile widened.

"And how often have you rehearsed that one?" he said, looking at Nick knowingly.

Nick wasn't sure how to respond to that and was now becoming uneasy with the strange man's presence.

"Not sure what you mean by that, Mr...."

The man waved a dismissive hand.

"Not important now, Nick. I know for a fact that's the least pressing of your questions."

Nick took a step back.

"Who are you, and how do you know my name?"

The Dark Man stood tall and straight, an arrogant gleam in his eyes.

"I know a lot about you, Nick. More than you do, I'd wager."

The man took a step forward, and Nick took another step back. Blitz was now hiding beneath the bushes far away, still growling.

"Like, for instance, that you can do things you can't explain. Like move faster than an ordinary man. Jump higher. Heal quicker. That sort of thing."

The man kept approaching. Nick put a hand on his sword.

"You're luckier than most. Bullets fly past you. The police never catch you. Almost as if you were…protected…by something."

Nick stood his ground. Thankfully, the man stopped his approach, but Nick still couldn't help but feel somewhat helpless before the weight of the man's knowledge.

"And I'd be willing to wager that there's something inside of you. A voice or a sensation. One that calls to you. As if you have a purpose you can't quite remember."

Nick suddenly found it difficult to stand.

"How could you know that?" he said.

"Because, Nick," the dark man responded. "I know what you are."

He then turned around, and began walking back down the path from whence he had come.

"Wait!" Nick yelled.

The Dark Man turned and smiled.

"I'll be in touch. And then you and I will have a lot to talk about," he said.

He did something then that made Nick's heart nearly stop in his chest.

The Dark Man took to the air, literally flying off the ground and into the night sky. His cloak flapped in the breeze, and in seconds he was gone.

Nick plopped to the ground, the strength suddenly absent from his legs, but it was not the man's supernatural exit that left Nick reeling.

He knew. He said he knew what Nick was.

Blitz trotted over to Nick's side and licked his hand, but Nick barely felt it.

Weird night, indeed.

7

Melissa had just finished packing. Jason was downstairs cooking them a quick breakfast before they hit the road. It was going to be a long day. First a five-hour drive on Melissa's Harley to Alabama, then a trip to discover if her father still even lived in the same ramshackle crap hole she had left him in, followed by, if he was still there…the most difficult confrontation of her life.

But it needed to be done. Her breakdown the other night had convinced her that there were a few demons of her own that Melissa needed to put to rest. If she could not find her uncle, she would have to settle for her father.

She came to the top of the stairs, headed for Stacy's room so she could say goodbye when suddenly she heard Stacy cry out. Melissa ran the last few steps, wondering if her thoughts about demons hadn't brought a real one.

But Stacy was alone in her bed. Melissa stood in the doorway and watched as she writhed and bucked beneath the sheets as if fighting something. Her face was contorted in a grimace of pain and anger. Just a bad dream, but it looked like a doozy.

She walked over to Stacy's bed and sat down beside her, grabbing the girl by the shoulders and gently shaking her.

Stacy cried out again, this time with more volume and a lot more anger. She swiped at Melissa with her fingernails, and Melissa gritted her teeth as Stacy left a long scratch on her arm.

"No!" Stacy screamed. "Leave me alone!"

Melissa thought for a moment of doing just that. Let the girl have her nightmare. What did she care? But then she looked at Stacy's face again, her dark hair flowing wildly over her forehead, her skin glistening with sweat and her fingers tensed like claws. This wasn't right. This wasn't Stacy.

So instead of letting her go, Melissa pulled her close and held her. She let Stacy struggle and whimper, and she whispered in her ear in an attempt to calm her, just as Jason had done to her several days before.

"It's okay, kiddo. It's just a dream. Whatever it is, I won't let it hurt you."

Stacy bucked a couple of more times, but Melissa felt her go a little more limp, and the sounds coming from her mouth started to sound less angry and more helpless.

"Now wake up. Shake it off and come back to us."

Stacy whimpered one more time, and then Melissa felt her begin to hold her back, almost frantically, like a child holding onto a parent in a time of fear and confusion.

She opened her eyes and leaned back, and Melissa immediately saw the disorientation in them.

"Melissa?" she said weakly. "What's going on?"

"You were having a nightmare. Must have been pretty intense, too. You looked like you wanted to claw someone's eyes out."

Stacy lay back on the bed and pushed the hair out of her face.

"Yeah. I think, someone was trying to tell me something. Make me feel something I didn't want to feel."

"Who?" Melissa asked.

"I...don't remember," Stacy answered. "I almost do...but it's gone."

"Doesn't matter, then. It's over." Melissa said, trying to sound comforting.

The look on Stacy's face told her it didn't work. Whatever the dream had been, it was still lingering inside of her.

"I think I've had that dream before. A few times. I always wake up feeling angry at nothing and ashamed at myself for reasons I can't remember."

"Oh yeah? Princess Sunshine angry at something? What has the world come to?" Melissa said with a wry smile.

Stacy kicked her in the leg but giggled a little.

"Jerk."

"Well...now that that's settled, I'm off to see the wizard. Jason and I are having a quick bite and then we're out of here. I just came to say goodbye," Melissa said, putting the business of Stacy's dream out of her mind.

"I wish I could go with you," Stacy said. "This is a pretty big deal, you confronting your father after all this time."

Melissa shrugged. "It really hasn't been that long. But yeah...seems like forever. Jason'll be there for me, and besides, who would watch after Mr. Hero if we all left? The jackass spends so much time jumping between buildings and examining his own psyche that he can't even tie his own shoes half the time."

That got Stacy laughing. Melissa laughed a little as well, relieved to see her friend back to her normal self again.

"I can't be Nick's babysitter all the time," Stacy said.

"Oh, no? You seem to relish the job."

Stacy rolled her eyes and muttered something under her breath.

Melissa laughed again.

"All right, kiddo. I'm out of here. Tell Nick I said goodbye when he drags his skinny ass back in from doing his hero crap."

"Will do," Stacy nodded.

"And no more bad dreams, okay?" Melissa said as she got off the bed and headed towards the door.

"Okay. And Melissa?" Stacy called after her.

Melissa turned around and looked at Stacy quizzically.

"Thanks," Stacy said, smiling softly.

The site of it warmed Melissa's heart a bit. She did care for the girl, even if she did think of her as a burden half the time.

"Any time. Later gator."

"After a while, crocodile," Stacy replied, waving as Melissa left the room.

A few hours later Melissa was feeling the wind whip through her hair and asphalt grind by beneath the wheels of her motorcycle. Jason held on firmly behind her, comforting her, if only a little.

Her heart was beating so fast it was difficult to keep her attention on the road. What lay ahead of her was worse than any enemy, any thug, or any physical threat Melissa had ever faced. She was almost there. Soon she would be doing something she swore long ago she would never have to do. She was going to confront her past.

She didn't really know what her father would say. Whatever it was, it wasn't likely to be pleasant. She was prepared for that. What she wasn't prepared for was the shame and fear he would likely hold for her. She had, after all, beaten him to a pulp the last time she saw him.

She wasn't looking for a fight. She didn't want to hurt him more than she already had. In fact, she wasn't entirely sure what she did want out of this confrontation. Perhaps she wanted a better final memory of him. Perhaps she wanted to see her childhood home one last time. Or perhaps…she just wanted to ask him why.

Melissa thought that last possibility the most likely. He had made her life a living hell from the moment her mother died to the moment she left him. Every opportunity he had, he made her feel like dirt - less than a person - an insignificant waste of space. She had proven him wrong, but somehow, all these years later, that proof no longer felt like a victory. In fact, part of her wondered if she hadn't taken the easy way out.

If she hadn't left that day…in the way that she had…she would not have condemned herself to a life on the road - a life of conflict and pain, of loneliness and apathy. It wasn't until she met Jason that she had allowed herself to feel again. Fighting had been the only thing that made her feel alive, but now her friends had given her a whole new reason to live. In a way, they had given her back a piece of the person she was when her mother was still alive. Innocent, and ready to hope.

She wanted him to see that. She didn't know what it would accomplish, but she wanted him to, nonetheless.

They arrived in the mid-afternoon, pulling into a gravel driveway that hadn't seemed to have changed in the five years since she had been gone. The house didn't look terribly different either. It was still the same shabby pre-fabricated home Melissa had spent her childhood in. Good times and bad. Wonderful memories and terrible ones.

She parked her bike, but made no motion to dismount. Jason did, and looked at her patiently.

"It's just a house, Melissa. And whoever is inside of it is just a man."

She fought to catch her breath. She wanted to look at Jason for comfort, but she couldn't tear her eyes off of the place. Its windows seemed to stare back at her accusingly, as if to remind her of the violence that had occurred the last time she walked away from them.

There was a car in the driveway. Perhaps her father's, though not one she recognized. Finally, she made herself get off the bike and take a step towards the front door.

The next steps came easier, and by the time she and Jason had reached the doorstep, Melissa realized she was operating entirely on auto-pilot.

She pushed the doorbell. The familiar buzz made her heart leap into her throat again.

They heard footsteps on the other side of the door. Jason put a hand on her shoulder. She barely felt it.

But when the door opened, it was not her father standing there, but a middle-aged woman in a yellow floral dress.

"May I help you?" she asked.

Melissa opened her mouth and was suddenly terrified that no sound would come out of it no matter how hard she tried.

"I'm looking for Bart Moonbeam. I'm...his daughter," Melissa finally managed, surprised to hear the words coming out of her mouth.

The woman's face wrinkled up in confusion for a moment.

"Moonbeam...oh, that's right...Bart had a different last name when he was younger. I know him as Bart Moon."

Moon. So he had changed his name back. When they got married, Melissa's parents, in true new age fashion, had altered their last name. Moon became Moonbeam.

"And you're his...daughter, you say?" the woman continued.

Melissa swallowed, then nodded.

"Yes, he did mention you from time to time."

"Where is he now?" Jason asked, trying to pry the pertinent information out of the woman.

"Ah, well, you see..." the woman stammered. "I'm his live-in nurse. Bart's been in bad health for the past couple of years and...a few days ago he had another heart attack. The doctor's don't think he's going to recover from this one. He's in the hospital down at St. Bend."

Melissa took a step back. She sighed heavily. The breath releasing from her lungs felt laced with both relief and sadness.

"You should go see him, dear. I'm just packing up some of his things. There was always too much junk in this house, but he would never let me touch any of it until now."

Melissa looked back up at her.

"I haven't seen my father in...a very long time. You seem like you know him pretty well. What...what kind of life has he had?"

The woman seemed a bit taken aback by the question.

53

"A sad one, my dear. Bart did little but sit on his duff and talk to me about his wife. Your mother, rest her soul. From what I've heard of her, she seemed like an angel."

Melissa smiled a little.

"Thank you."

The woman nodded, returning her smile.

"I've heard he was an alcoholic years ago, but I never saw him drink. No, he just wandered around the house, talking to me and to himself. Like he was searching for something he knew he would never find."

Melissa felt a stab of pain in her chest.

"He talked about your mother, and occasionally he talked about you. Sometimes he'd tell me about the things he regretted. Apparently he did something terrible years ago, when he and your mother were young, but he would never tell me what."

Melissa had no idea what the woman could be talking about, but she imagined that the Bart Moonbeam she knew, formerly-and-now-once-again Bart Moon, had done a lot of things in his life worth regretting. When she was around him, it seemed the thing that he regretted most of all was fathering her.

The thought steeled her resolve.

"We'll go to the hospital, then. Thanks for talking to us."

"Oh do be careful, Melissa," the woman said. "Yes, I remember your name. Your father is in pretty bad shape right now. If you came here for a confrontation, now might not be the right time."

Melissa felt the irony of the statement. If what the woman said was true, it might be the only time.

"I just want to see him. It's been a long time and I wanted to know how he's been."

The woman seemed to warm up a bit at that.

"Then that should be alright, dear. Just don't get him too excited, and tell him Betty says to keep drinking lots of water!"

Melissa nodded.

"Thanks, Betty. Oh, and I might want to stop by the house again after I go the hospital. There might be some things in there worth hanging on to."

"I'll be here," Betty said.

Melissa and Jason said goodbye to the woman after getting directions to the hospital.

54

"I'm sorry to hear about his condition, Melissa," Jason said. "I know this isn't what you expected."

"I don't know what I expected, really - and I don't know if this is going to make things easier or harder."

She revved her motorcycle and rolled back down the driveway.

"Only one way to find out."

Somehow, walking into the hospital at St. Bend was easier than pulling into the driveway of her old house. She had come this far. She had seen her past in front of her. She was frightened, but striding down the cold, echoing halls of the hospital, she seemed to gain purpose and resolve with each step.

All of that faded when she reached the doorway of room 204, the room the nurse downstairs had directed them to.

Her father lay there, looking old, haggard, and beaten - with an IV attached to his arm and several machines beeping away by his bedside. His eyes were mercifully closed. She didn't know if she was ready for him to see her yet.

Standing in that doorway she suddenly felt as if it were she who had put him there. As if that beating years ago had left him bed-ridden and crippled. As if her actions had taken the last bit of vitality from him and left him an invalid.

Becoming aware of her presence, Bart Moon opened his eyes and glanced towards the doorway.

She saw them widen. His eyes filled with bewilderment and surprise. His chest rose and fell a little faster. And then his whole body seemed to become more rigid. His eyes narrowed a bit, and he looked away.

"It's you," he said to her.

His voice hit Melissa like a javelin in her gut. Never mind the cold tone of his words; just his voice itself made her want to curl up and cry.

"Hi, Dad," she managed in a weak, quiet voice.

Jason nudged her a bit, and the two of them walked into the room. He stood by the door, closing it behind him, while Melissa approached her father's bedside.

Bart didn't look at her as she stood over him. She could see that his fists were clenched, though she didn't know if that were from anger or discomfort or both.

"Why are you here, girl? Come to look down at your shit-stain of a father one last time before he kicks the bucket?"

She had tried to prepare herself for words like those, but hearing them still hurt a little.

"No, Dad. I...I just wanted to see you again. I didn't know you were sick."

He continued to stare out the window on the far wall. The late afternoon sun shone brightly on his face. He needed a shave. Melissa cursed herself for noticing such intimate details.

"So Betty told you?" he said. "How is she?"

"Fine. She was tidying the place up a bit when we got there. She seems nice," Melissa added, hoping to encourage her father to open up about the true nature of his relationship to the woman.

Instead, he looked over at Jason.

"She's probably stealing my stuff. Who's he?"

Melissa turned to Jason. He winked at her. For once, he wasn't wearing his glasses.

"That's Jason, Dad. He's my best friend."

"Hmph," Bart mumbled. "I kinda figured you'd shacked up with a nigger."

Melissa took a step back.

"Don't say that...don't you dare," she said sternly. She didn't care how sick he was. Her father would not insult Jason.

She glanced behind her shoulder and gave him an apologetic look. Jason just shook his head and made a dismissive motion with his hand.

"Your daughter and I are just friends, Mr. Moon. I came here to support her. Seeing you again was a big deal. It took a lot of guts - and let me tell you, I've never met anyone with more guts than your daughter."

Melissa smiled warmly at Jason before turning back to her father. This time he was looking back at her.

"Guts," he said mockingly. "Is that what they call it when you beat up an old man and run away with his money?"

"Dad," Melissa said, feeling the anger well up within her. "I didn't do anything to you that you didn't have coming."

"Fuck you," he said, turning away from her again.

She felt the flood gates of anger opening - and had no desire to stop them.

56

"You hit me," she said between gritted teeth, "so many times… You hurt me when you were drunk. You hurt me when you were hung-over. You hurt me when you were just plain bored. Every word out of your mouth was, 'why couldn't you' this and 'why did you have to do that.' You let a psychotic child molester do things to me I will never recover from."

For an instant, his browed clenched up and the anger in his eyes was replaced with something else. Regret? Melissa did not give herself time to wonder, for she had one more thing left to say.

"But do you know what hurt most of all… Bart? The fact that you blamed me for Mom. You blamed me for the fact that you lost her. She died and left us and it was my fault."

She felt her hot cheeks become wet with tears. She didn't realize she had started crying. She didn't care.

"I lost her, too!" she screamed with all the venom and bitterness that had dwelled inside of her like a puss-filled wound for years of her wasted life.

With those words said, the room became eerily silent. With her rage vented, all she could feel was sadness. And now she truly could see that she had left him broken a second time. There was no fight left in this man. His eyes were welled up with tears not unlike her own.

"I loved her more than anything I've ever loved in all the years I've lived. And I know that I could never love anything…ever…as much or as deeply," she said through those tears.

All the anger was gone. What was left was pity, both towards the shell of a man before her, and towards herself - the incomplete human being his neglect and her mother's death had made her. The rage-addicted, reckless, irresponsible, emotionally broken individual she had allowed herself to become.

Like father, like daughter.

"But you know what, Dad? I loved you, too."

She watched a tear roll down his cheek. The anger was returning to his face, but she didn't care. She had to tell him. Even the things she hadn't dared to tell herself.

"I loved you and I trusted you like any little girl would have. You were my Daddy. And with Mom gone, you were all I had. We had each other. We both loved her more than anything. I know that. And that love should have made us stronger…instead of…this."

She wiped a tear from her cheek.

"When you started hitting me, and blaming me for what happened…it broke my heart all over again. Every time you looked at me with that…hatred in your eyes, another part of that little girl died, too. Until it was all gone and replaced with the anger you saw that day I left."

The tears were gone from his eyes. He was only angry now, she could see that.

"You should have loved me, too," she finished, wiping another tear from her face.

He turned those angry eyes back to her.

"How dare you," he said. "How dare you think that you're the victim."

She shouldn't have been surprised by those words, but somehow she still was.

"I loved your mother more than I could ever say. More than myself. More than my life. More than anything. Life kept trying to fuck that up, but I kept fixing it. Until you came along," he said, his eyes pointing at her like daggers.

"I couldn't fix you. You know why? Because you were a part of us both. A part of her and a part of me. If I took you away, it would have killed us. So I put up with you. And do you know how she repaid me? By loving you more."

Melissa felt her breath hitch in her throat.

"It was supposed to be just her and I. Her and I forever. And then you came along and took that from me. You stole her love. You stole our happiness. And when she died…all I had left was you. A living, breathing reminder of what I had lost."

She could feel his words digging into her, and her heart beat so fast she thought it would leap out of her chest.

"I didn't kill her, Dad. Mom had cancer. She loved us both till the day she died. You were with her when it happened. You had to know. You had to have seen that she loved you, too."

He turned away from her again, the anger replaced by weariness.

"Just get out of here."

Melissa looked at him for a moment more and then nodded. She had said what she meant to say. There was no more reason for her to be here. When she turned back to Jason, she saw him sitting in a chair against the wall, his face propped up in his hands and his eyes filled with sadness at the scene that had just played out before him. He looked up at her and stood while she walked towards him. They both stopped when they heard her father's voice again.

"Melissa," he said softly, his face still turned away. "I'm sorry."

She froze. Her head cocked to the side a bit. Had she just heard him right?

"I'm sorry for bringing you into this fucked up world."

Melissa felt her fist clench beside her. At that moment she didn't know whether to be angry at him or to mourn the relationship with him she had never really had.

"I'm sorry too, Daddy."

He rolled over, turning his back to them, and didn't say another word.

When they reached the parking lot, Melissa crumbled. Her legs went out from under her, and Jason eased her to the sidewalk. He held her as she cried and screamed and writhed with all the weight of years of sadness and loss. She mourned the happiness she had left behind as a child. The love of a father she had never really received. The self-respect she had abandoned the day she had left him behind. It was all gone now.

For nearly half an hour they sat there, with Jason rocking her and people pretending not to look as they walked to their cars.

The past was gone, Melissa knew. Truly gone now. She had said goodbye to her father for real this time. The only way she could look now was forward.

She looked up at Jason. His light brown eyes looked back at her.

Without thinking, Melissa kissed him.

It only lasted a moment, but it was all the two of them needed.

When it was done, she could see the shock in his eyes. She sensed him wanting to ask why, but he didn't dare. He had the feeling he didn't want to look a gift horse in the mouth.

"I needed you today, Jason. I needed you and you were there."

He smiled. "I always will be."

His words filled her back up a bit, and she smiled back.

"I know."

She looked at him and remembered the way she used to feel back in the days when she felt trapped in that house with her innocence behind her and nothing but what appeared to be a life of abuse and pain in front of her.

"I wanted it all to go away, Jason. My dad, my uncle, everyone and everything. I wanted it all to burn. More than that, I wanted to be the one to burn it."

Jason said nothing, but couldn't help but feel uncomfortable at the tone in her voice.

"The whole world," she said, looking down at the pavement. In her eyes wasn't anger or fear or sadness now, only memory.

"The world is so full of hate, Jason. Maybe that's what drove me to Raven. That's the way he was. He accepted that hate. Hell, he encouraged it. When I met him, I believed that kindness was a lie, compassion a bullshit excuse to get close to people so you could take from them...."

"You're not like Raven," Jason argued.

"Aren't I? I'm sure as hell not like Nick or Stacy...or you. I don't look for good in the world because I know it's not there. I wanted it all to go away. Everyone and everything."

She looked up at him and gently caressed his cheek.

"I still do."

Jason placed his hand over hers.

"Everyone but us...needs to burn."

She stood up without saying another word, and he stood with her. She could tell he didn't know how to respond to that.

Melissa felt a kind of release then. She wasn't what Nick was. She would never be. She wasn't a hero and didn't care to be one. She was selfish and she was okay with that. All that mattered was the little family she had carved out for herself. Unlike so many other things in the world, it was truly hers. The rest of the world could burn.

Holding Jason's hand the entire way, Melissa walked back to her bike. There was one more thing to say goodbye to before they returned home.

Looking at Jason, she felt immeasurable gratitude that she could finally say that again.

Home.

Betty was sitting on a bench in front of the house when they got back, having a smoke. There was something odd about seeing the demure, soft-spoken woman with a cigarette in her mouth, but Jason supposed she had to have some toughness hidden away to put up with Melissa's father.

She waved them over and stamped out her cigarette on the ground.

"How is he?"

Getting off the bike, Melissa and Jason walked over to her. Melissa crossed her arms over her chest and looked at the dirt where the cigarette now lay.

"He's sick. I can tell. But he was well enough to talk to us. And he's…pretty much the same as I remember him," Melissa said.

"A bitter old man obsessed with the past," Betty replied.

Melissa nodded.

"I can tell by the redness in your eyes that much of what he had to say wasn't very nice."

Melissa looked up at her and then wiped her eyes again, as if that would help.

"I expected that. We never got along after Mom died."

Betty sighed.

"I'm sorry, dear. Bart was a good man, once. He had to have been to have loved your mother as much as he did. But it's very rare that he lets that good man out anymore. Usually he's content to be as miserable and as mean-spirited as he wants to be. As if spreading his pain around will somehow bring him justice for the wrongs life committed against him."

"You knew him pretty well," Jason commented.

Betty looked over at him, and he could see the sadness in her eyes.

"Yes, I did. When the hospital assigned me to him after his first heart attack, he fought me tooth and nail, but eventually…eventually he stopped fighting. He let me in, as much as a man like that could, and I got to see all the pain and anger that turns a good man into…that."

"I can tell you care for him," Melissa said. "Thank you. He needed that. I couldn't give it to him. He wouldn't let me. But I'm glad someone did."

Betty smiled sweetly.

"You're welcome, dear."

Jason wandered through the small house while Melissa and Betty dug through old boxes full of papers, photographs, and keepsakes from the past twenty years. He didn't want to bother them, because he could see how lost Melissa was in her trip down memory lane.

The back bedroom, obviously Bart's, was still a mess. He walked inside and glanced around at the piles of clothes, shuffled papers, and discarded cigarette cartons lying on the floor. He imagined that Bart hadn't let Betty clean this room as often because this was his personal sanctum. A man like that would defend his sanctuary to the death.

Beside the bed and next to a desk on the far wall was a safe - its door open wide and its contents still lying within. Perhaps Bart had been going through it when he had his heart attack, or perhaps the thing had not been closed in a long time. He walked over to it, suddenly curious as to what kind of things Bart Moon would deem important enough to keep in a safe in the wall.

It was papers, mostly. Property deeds, legal documents, an address book. He flipped through the address book, hoping to find mention of Melissa's uncle. If he ever knew how to find that man, Jason fully intended to track him down and rip his heart from his chest. David Moon's information wasn't there, though Jason saw that a page had been ripped from the book in about the place David's name would have fallen in the alphabet. Was the page ripped from the book out of anger? Did Bart regret what David had done to Melissa and the part he had played in allowing it to happen? Jason didn't know, though he imagined that such a thing was possible.

He noticed one other oddity in the address book. One of the entries had been marked over with a black marker. Jason could faintly make out a few words underneath the ink. The person's last name was Green. Their address was somewhere in Georgia.

Odd. If this were someone Bart had wanted to forget, why hadn't he ripped this page from the book as well?

Jason put the question aside and placed the address book back in the safe. There was a small pile of pictures in there that he was more interested in anyway. He picked them up and began flipping through them.

The first one was of Bart and Melissa's mother, Terra. Suddenly he could see why both Melissa and her father had spent so many years loving this woman. She was radiantly beautiful in a way Jason had never seen before. Her hair was long and golden, a shade lighter than Melissa's. Her eyes were light green and filled with a welcoming warmth. Her smile nearly took Jason's breath away. It was wide and joyful and unapologetic. In the rare instances when she allowed it to happen, Melissa had that exact same smile.

"Wow," Jason commented to himself, and flipped to the next picture. There were a few more of Terra and a young Bart, looking more care-free and happy than Jason would have thought possible after meeting the man. Then there were several of the two of them with a young Melissa.

Jason laughed to himself as he took in the sight of what must have been the four-or-five-year-old version of his best friend. She had a wide, mischievous grin sporting a few crooked teeth. Her hair was a little lighter then, almost like her mother's. In every picture her arms were wrapped around either Terra or Bart - usually her mother.

Jason's mirth faded a bit when he got to the last picture. It showed Melissa sitting on her father's broad shoulder, grinning away and waving at the camera. On Bart's other shoulder sat a little boy. He was smaller than Melissa. Thin and pale, almost sickly. His hair was light brown and wavy, and his eyes were green like Terra's. He smiled happily.

There was something about this picture that made Jason very uneasy.

He flipped the picture over. Scrawled on the bottom of the back in blue ink were the words, "Melissa and Ronnie."

Who was Ronnie?

He flipped the picture back to the front again. A cold chill went up his spine the moment the little boy's eyes peered up at him again. The longer he looked, the more uncomfortable Jason felt.

Jason shook his head. It was just a little boy. A happy little boy, from the look of it. Maybe a cousin or a neighbor. Aside from the eyes, he didn't really bear any family resemblance, so Jason didn't think it was more than that.

He started to put the picture down but hesitated before releasing it. He found himself, uneasy as he was, wanting to look at it just a moment longer, as if studying it would reveal to him the source of that discomfort.

So Jason put the picture in his pocket, resolving to ask Melissa about it later. She would likely have a simple answer as to who the boy was, and that would be that. Mystery solved.

As he put the other pictures down, he noticed a glint of metal peeking out from beneath the stack of papers. It looked like a chain.

He looped his finger around it and pulled. What came out was a small golden locket attached to a gold chain. It was the kind you can open, he noticed, so he flipped the clasp and swung open the hinge.

He gasped a little.

On one side of the locket was Terra, with that same radiant, gorgeous smile he had seen before. Any man alive could have fallen in love with that smile. Jason himself would have fallen in love with it, if not for what was on the other side of the locket.

Staring out at him, her big blue eyes gleaming, was Melissa. She couldn't have been more than seven or eight. The little girl who would one day be the woman he now knew looked up at whoever was taking the picture with that kind of perfect, unconditional love only a child can give.

He closed the locket again. He looked at it, hanging on its gold chain, for a moment, and then put it in his pocket as well.

If Bart asked for it back, he would give it. Otherwise, Jason felt that there was someone who deserved it more.

A couple of hours later, Jason and Melissa said their goodbyes to Betty. They exchanged numbers so Betty could keep Melissa posted on Bart's condition. Melissa gave her a big hug before climbing on her bike. She squeezed Jason's hand while she looked at her old house one last time. Her eyes lingered on its tired old frame for a few moments, and then she nodded, revving her bike and pulling out of the driveway.

Before leaving town, the two of them stopped at a motel to crash for the evening. Melissa hadn't thought it right to stay at the house. Jason didn't blame her. It had been a very long day, and there were far too many memories there.

Finishing up their late dinner, which consisted of cheap fast food, Jason suddenly remembered the picture he wanted to ask her about.

"Melissa, I found something in your dad's room I wanted to ask you about," he said, handing her the picture.

"Who's Ronnie?"

Melissa, sitting Indian style on one of the two motel beds, took the picture from him. She took a deep breath when she saw the picture. He thought he saw her eyes well up for a moment, but then it was gone. Finally, she gave it back to him.

"Ronnie was my cousin. He stayed with us for a while when I was little. A summer one year. He was sick. Kids picked on him. His parents were jerks. I think he was only really happy with us. I remember...I promised him it would be okay, that the world wouldn't get the best of him. Eventually he went back to live with his parents and passed away soon after. He had some sort of heart disease, I think."

"I'm sorry," Jason said, feeling a bit relieved that the simplest answer had turned out to be the right one, but still saddened by the tale.

"It must have been hard on you, being that young. You were close, huh?"

Melissa nodded, taking one last bite of her cheeseburger before crumpling up the wrapper.

"Yeah. I remember crying for days when Dad told me Ronnie died. Felt like I broke my promise. Mom cried a lot, too."

"Hmm," Jason muttered, remembering the resemblance between Ronnie's eyes and Terra's.

"Was he your cousin on your mom's side or your dad's?"

"My mom's," Melissa answered, and Jason saw her shudder. "I don't think that sleazeball David ever had any children, thank God. Wouldn't want to think of what would have happened to them if he did."

"So what were your aunt and uncle on your mom's side like?" Jason asked, changing the subject away from David for both of their sakes.

"Don't know," she said, shaking her head and shrugging. "Never met them."

With that she swiped the trash off the bed and stretched out.

"Could you get the light? Now that my stomach's full I think I need to pass out for a few hours," she said.

65

Jason nodded and switched off the light. After putting away his own trash and picking up Melissa's, he climbed into his own bed.

"Thanks again for today, Jason," she said to him.

"You're welcome. Couldn't let you face your demons alone," he answered.

"Good. Now we've got to start working on yours...and Nick's," she added with a chuckle.

"Yeah," he replied. Before he could think of anything else to say, Jason heard a small snore emanate from the dark to his right. Exhaustion had finally caught up to her.

He listened to her for a while, part of him wishing that snore were a little closer. Perhaps right next to him. Maybe even in his arms.

Kissing her earlier had proven to him that his feelings for her were there to stay. Raven's captivity hadn't killed them, and he doubted anything else could either.

But it had apparently been just a kiss - an act of gratitude from a girl who needed comfort. He couldn't fault her for that. He wouldn't let his feelings be a burden to her. She had enough of those.

Jason slowed down his breathing and began forcing himself to fall asleep, a trick he had developed in Raven's dark cell. The best way to deal with unnecessary feelings was to ignore them, and for both of their sakes, that was exactly what Jason decided to do.

Before he dozed off, an image of Melissa's cousin Ronnie flashed briefly into his mind - and for an instant, he almost had it. The reason the picture of the small boy made him so uneasy. But then it was gone again. So Jason decided to ignore that, too - for now.

He fell asleep to the sound of Melissa's snore. The sound of it put a small smile on his face.

8

Nick leaned against the brick building, trying to be as much of a wallflower as he could be. Dozens of people walked by him in both directions - tourists carrying shopping bags - locals shambling from one place to the next with a certain carelessness that only a resident of New Orleans could convey. Nick supposed that "carelessness" wasn't really the right word. They just didn't seem to notice their surroundings much. He wondered if it was the same in New York or Los Angeles or any other city where the rich and poor intermingled constantly.

Then again, he was standing in the French Quarter. In addition to being the most popular part of town, it was also the weirdest. Nick kind of liked it.

He heard the bell jingle behind him. He barely had time to turn around before Stacy jumped into his arms.

"Hey!" he exclaimed. "What if I hadn't caught you?"

She shrugged happily.

"Never even crossed my mind."

Nick shook his head but couldn't help but smile.

"So what's the verdict?" he asked. Stacy had asked him to wait for her while she went for a check-up at the local clinic. She hadn't been sleeping well lately and wanted to make sure she wasn't coming down with something.

"Fit as a fiddle," she replied. "In fact, he says I'm in better shape than most girls my age. And I have nicer legs, and a cuter...."

"Can it," Nick said, rolling his eyes. "So am I going to have to carry you around all night?"

"Yep," Stacy giggled.

"Fine," he said. "That just means you're buying dinner."

For the next two hours, Nick and Stacy sat at their favorite outdoor café, chatting about New Orleans, places they'd like to travel (though Nick honestly didn't know where he had been and where he hadn't) and absent friends.

67

"So what do you want to do, Nick? When everything's settled? When The Whisper is gone and you've got your memories back and there's nothing left to fight and no one left to save? What then? What do you want for you?" she asked him, her brown eyes staring intently into his hazel ones.

Nick thought for a moment. It was a question he had tried asking himself before but one he never really knew how to answer. There would always be something to fight, wouldn't there? There would always be people to save. He was almost afraid of wondering what life would be like after The Pull, for fear of what was at the end of it.

"A cabin - in the mountains. A place to wake up every day and just…live. No struggle. No stress. Just me, Blitz, and all of you."

"All of us?" she prodded.

"Yeah. You, Melissa, Jason, maybe even Patricia and Benjamin."

"Crowded cabin," she said with a smile.

"We'll make it a big one," he replied.

"What about you?" he asked. "If you weren't tagging along with rejects like us, where would you want to be?"

She leaned back in her chair and stretched her arms behind her head.

"You, me, a hotel room by the beach. Really good room service."

Nick burst out laughing. That was the most forward Stacy had ever been, and he couldn't contain himself.

He looked up to make sure he hadn't offended her, but she was smiling.

"You're terrible," he said.

She leaned forward, placing her hands close to his on the table.

"I just know what would make me happy."

Nick smiled but began feeling a little uncomfortable. Stacy had always been a little flirtatious with him, but this was different. This wasn't like her.

He glanced around, hoping for some ammunition to change the subject.

She followed his gaze.

"What are you looking at?" she asked.

"Come with me," he said, grabbing her hand and throwing some money on the table.

With lots of whispers and giggles, the two of them climbed a service ladder behind a building across from the restaurant.

"So, are we going to make out or throw water balloons at people?" she asked him when they were on the roof.

"Not quite," he said, grabbing her hand.

"Just do as I do," he added with a wink.

Stacy looked at him curiously, and then her breath caught in her throat when he started running towards the edge of the roof, still holding her hand.

"Nick..." she said, suddenly very worried.

"Trust me," he said. "And you might want to..."

They were approaching the gap between this building and the next.

"...jump!!!"

Stacy let out a small scream, but jumped just like he did. She felt the wind whip by her as they leaped through the air and then the crunch of her feet hitting the next rooftop over.

She squealed happily when they landed, and Nick laughed. However, he was still holding her hand, and he was still running.

She laughed with him as they ran to the edge again, and then jumped to the next building...and then the next...and then the next.

It was like being in a ballet. After a while she let go of his hand and just started letting her own body do what it wanted. She found herself grinning uncontrollably and gasping like a six-year-old on a roller coaster every time she took to the air.

The gaps between buildings were admittedly small on this street. No more than three or four feet max, and yet Stacy still felt as if they were flying.

Nick was moving so effortlessly, and beside him, she felt just as graceful as he was.

She had never felt so free in her life.

Eventually Nick stopped in front of her, and swept her up into his arms, twirling her around and letting her momentum turn their movement into a dance.

He was laughing. She was laughing. He held her there, a little off the ground, with her face just inches above his and his arms so tight around her.

And then he put her down, and Stacy finally felt like she could breathe again. She watched him walk over to the edge of the building and sit down, dangling his legs off the side. He didn't seem the least bit out of breath.

She walked over and sat beside him.

There was a group of young men dancing around a barrel below them. Someone had set a fire in the barrel, and the flames danced off the walls of the buildings nearby. Two of the men were playing trumpets, and the sound of jazz music echoed in the night.

"God, I love this city sometimes," Nick said, watching the festivities below.

"Yeah," she said, pushing some of her windswept hair out of her face.

He looked up at her.

"Didn't scare you, did I?"

She laughed, still a little out of breath.

"You about gave me a heart attack at first, but then…I just let go and trusted you and…"

He put his hand over hers and smiled warmly.

"And I've never felt so alive," she said, squeezing his hand back.

"Do you do that every time you're out here?" she asked.

Nick nodded. "Just about."

"Wow," she said.

"I've always wanted to bring you up here. To show you what it was like. Sometimes, when the world seems so dark and nothing makes any sense, I'll come up here and just…run," he said.

She looked up, noticing how bright the stars were.

"Wherever Jason and Melissa are, I hope they can see this," she said.

"Me too," Nick agreed, also looking upward.

She glanced at him, watching him as he gazed at the stars.

"You know I love you, Nick."

Even in the dark she could see the color drain from his face. He looked at her, his hand going rigid in hers.

But she didn't let go. She just stared into his eyes, letting her heart continue to express through them what she had just said.

And then, to her surprise, Nick leaned forward and kissed her. His hand wrapped around the back of her neck. His other arm went around her waist and pulled her close to him. She whimpered a little as she felt herself almost melting into his embrace. Her arms wrapped around his back, wanting to pull their bodies even closer together.

But then he stopped. He pulled away, and she could see the look of anguish on his face.

"I can't. I can't do this," he said, and got to his feet.

"Why?" she asked. "Why can't you? I thought you felt the same...."

He looked down at her for a moment and then did two things. Nick shook his head and then turned around and ran.

Stacy watched him vault off the side of the building. She didn't even bother to get up and see where he had gone. She knew that by the time she looked he would already be nowhere in sight.

Instead, she just placed her face in her hands, and cried silently as the flames continued to dance below her.

Nick watched her the entire way home. He watched her climb down the ladder off the roof. He watched her walk back through the French Quarter. He followed her as she drove home.

Her eyes were tear-streaked and empty. He had made her that way, and it broke his heart to know it.

Stacy could not know how he felt. If he allowed his love for her to be out in the open, it would mean far more danger for her than for any of the others. The Whisper wanted to hurt him. It knew it could do that best through his friends. If Nick openly loved a woman, then that woman would be the first to die.

And then there was The Pull. Even if Nick allowed himself to love Stacy, what would happen when he suddenly couldn't stay with her any longer? What if The Pull took him someplace she couldn't follow? She would be left heartbroken or worse.

It was better to hurt her now than to place her in harm's way in the future. He cared for her too much to let that happen. His feelings wouldn't change, but he could not allow her to know that.

She deserved better.

He sat outside the house for a while, giving her time to turn in for the night. When all the lights were off, Nick snuck inside, greeted Blitz quietly, and then went to check on her.

71

Her door was open, as it often was. She lay with her back to the door, wrapped tightly in her blankets. The slow rise and fall of her shoulders told him she was already asleep.

He wanted to kiss those shoulders. He wanted to hold her and tell her it was alright.

Instead, he opened his mouth and soundlessly mouthed the words that he really wanted to say.

"I love you, too," his lips said.

Nick then left her for the second time that night.

If he had stayed just a moment longer, he would have notice those shoulders rise and fall a little faster. He would have seen her toss and turn in her sleep, her face a mask of pain and fear, her fingernails digging into her sheets.

If he had stayed, he would have perhaps been a bit more prepared for what came next.

9

Raven stood on a catwalk, peering down at the factory floor below. Workers under his employ scurried about like ants, assembling and cataloging a massive collection of items that made Raven tingle with anticipation.

"Almost time," he said to himself.

While satisfied at the progress of his plan, Raven couldn't help but be frustrated that his mentor was not present to admire the work. The Dark Man hadn't been seen in days, and Raven thought he knew why. That damned boy. The Hero, as both The Dark Man and the press insisted on calling him. What a pathetic title. Someone might as well write about him in the paper and call him "The Villain."

This gave Raven a chuckle, mostly because the thought would probably turn out to be ironically prophetic.

He noticed someone climbing the stairs to join him. Byron - the bounty hunter, still wearing that odd Victorian-era jacket with the ruffled sleeves.

"Byron! What a surprise. Come to give me an update on our young friends?"

Byron was looking at the factory floor as well, an uncomfortable look on his face.

"Assault weapons. M-60s, AK-47s. Mostly guns that do not use non-lethal rounds. Not even the police are armed with these anymore. You've collected thousands of them."

Raven nodded. "The spoils of the Peace and Disarmament Act."

"Which you helped author and get pushed through the senate," Byron looked at him with distrust.

Raven simply smiled.

"Dare I ask what you plan on doing with enough guns to supply an army?"

"Not just one army, my friend," Raven said. He then laughed and clapped a hand onto Byron's shoulder.

"I thought someone like you would know that it's not in your contract to ask questions."

Byron nodded.

"Fair enough. And yes...I do come with news."

"So let's hear it," Raven said, ushering Byron to follow him into a small office adjoining the catwalk.

"We're not the only ones watching Miss Moonbeam and her friends," Byron said as soon as the door was closed and the din of the busy factory floor was left behind.

"I know," Raven replied. "My colleague...the one you met before with the magic tricks and the violent disposition...seems to have taken a liking to them. Particularly our little 'Hero'."

"Yes," Byron agreed. "we've seen the sorcerer. But that's not who I'm referring to."

Raven leaned against a desk, still feeling a twinge of pain in his hip.

"Oh?"

Byron seemed unsure how to continue.

"About a week ago, Bitch and Brick were running surveillance on the lake house when they noticed something in the trees - something big. At the time, they couldn't tell what it was, but it was obviously humanoid and obviously keeping an eye on the house just as we were."

"Humanoid?" Raven asked with a raised eyebrow.

"Two nights later Brick and I were following Nick through the streets of the city. We split up. He was attacked by something."

Raven sat down behind the desk, his interest piqued.

"He says it was a monster. A huge metal man-shaped thing with claws as long as swords. He said it was strong and he said it was fast. He only got off one shot before the thing had him on the ground and bleeding from three different stab wounds. Thankfully minor. Whatever it was, I believe it just wanted to warn him off."

"Warn him off? You mean it was following Nick, too? Protecting him?"

Byron shook his head.

"Not protecting, Mr. Raven. Stalking. Whatever that thing is, it means them all harm. I've ordered my men to steer clear of the monster, but I've come to you for two reasons. The first is so you can warn your associate that he may be in danger if he continues to follow the boy."

Raven snickered.

"My associate can more than take care of himself, as you should have noticed."

"Nevertheless," Byron continued. "whatever the monster is, it is not of this world. I've seen similar things before. Based on Brick's description, I believe I know what it is. The Germans call them 'Einwohner.' You may have heard of them referred to as 'golems.' Empty shells filled with demonic spirits and sent after individuals at the behest of a cult or summoner."

Raven listened intently. Years ago he would have laughed at such a claim, but lately, he was beginning to see that there was a lot more to the world than met the eye.

"So you think someone summoned this thing to accost Nick?"

Byron shook his head once more.

"No. I think this one is operating of its own devices - which makes it much more dangerous. And now I must address my second reason for coming here, Mr. Raven."

Byron leaned forward, placing his hands on the desk and looking Raven square in the eye. For a moment, Raven feared the man meant to attack him, so intense was the gaze from his scarred face.

"What do we need to know about those young men and women that you haven't already told us?"

Raven rocked back and forth for a moment in his chair, keeping Byron's gaze. Truth was, he knew little more than Byron. All he had to go on was his own experience with the frustrating youths and his mentor's word that the boy, Nick, was the key to what was to come.

"You know about demons and monsters, apparently." Raven finally stated.

Bryon nodded slowly.

"I have seen many things in this world. Many of which defy the laws of man. I know that there is little which is not possible, and I know that many of man's worst nightmares are not nightmares at all, but cold hard truth."

Raven gave an approving nod.

"Then you would have little trouble believing that Nick...our little masked do-gooder, is a bit...special."

Byron stood back and crossed his arms over his chest.

"I've witnessed him do things that most men cannot do. I say most men, however. He does have remarkable talent, but I do not believe he is anything more than human."

Raven shrugged.

"Maybe. Nevertheless, he has power. My associate believes he may be the harbinger of something. An 'Einwohner' himself, in a way. Human, yes, but filled with something more. Obviously, if your stories of this 'monster' are true, we're not the only ones to think so."

Bryon stood silently and took in Raven's words. He then turned to look back out onto the factory floor below them.

"A harbinger, you say? For good or ill?"

Raven smiled.

"I believe that's what my associate is trying to find out."

Byron stood quietly for a moment longer before speaking.

"And what about you, Mr. Raven? What do you intend to be a harbinger of?"

Raven smiled, getting to his feet and walking slowly over to Byron's side. He looked down at the weapons laid out below them.

"Change, Byron," he said. "Global, irreversible change."

Byron looked at him. The unease was palpable in his steel-grey eyes.

"Nick is not the only one with power, Raven. You have it as well. And whatever he may be, I find myself somehow much more afraid of you."

With that, Byron opened the office door and proceeded down the catwalk, walking away without looking back.

Raven watched him go, a small smile on his face.

"You won't be the only one," he said quietly.

Nick spent the rest of that night back out on the streets, wandering around feeling more lost than ever. A couple of times he thought he noticed someone watching him. Someone tall and dressed in black. The older man from the other night, he suspected. Whoever the man was, he didn't seem interested in approaching Nick again just yet.

Right now, Nick didn't care. All he could think about was the image of Stacy lying in bed with her back turned to him, a telling gesture if there ever was one. He had blown it. He meant to, but that didn't make it sting any less. He had turned away from the girl he loved, and now she had every right to turn away from him.

He returned that morning to find Melissa and Jason back from Alabama. She was sitting on the couch, holding the phone to her ear. Her eyes were blank and her expression was far away. Jason nodded at him from the armchair when he came in.

"How did it go?" he asked Jason quietly.

"Good, actually. I'll tell you about it later. We just got back a few minutes ago. Stacy came downstairs and told Melissa that someone had been calling for her. I can only think of one person that would be, and it has me worried," Jason said.

Nick was about to ask who and why when Melissa hung up the phone.

"That was Betty," she said. "My dad passed away this morning."

The four of them sat at the kitchen table a bit later, Melissa and Jason cradling cups of warm coffee. Stacy sat with her arms crossed, making eye contact with no one. Nick watched Melissa expectantly. She had shown very little sign of emotion since the phone call. After hearing she and Jason recount what had happened to her in Alabama, Nick thought he understood why. She had already said goodbye to her father. His death just made it a bit more official.

"I'm not going to the funeral," Melissa said. "Betty told me there wouldn't be much of one anyway. And besides, he's getting cremated, just like Mom. Betty'll scatter his ashes in the same place we did hers."

"Are you sure you don't want to be there?" Jason asked.

Melissa shook her head.

"The last years of his life belonged to him and Betty. This is more for her than it would be for me."

"You saw him again. You closed that chapter of your life. That's all that really matters," Nick said.

Melissa gave him a weak smile and nodded.

"Yeah," she said, and Nick could see her eyes glisten for a moment with tears that suddenly wanted to come. But they didn't. Melissa just took a deep breath and continued to smile. It was a good kind of grief, Nick thought. A healthy kind.

He couldn't help but notice that Stacy hadn't said more than two words to Melissa since coming downstairs. She just sat there, her arms crossed tightly in front of her and her eyes locked on the table. She looked sad, but not once did she express her sorrow for Melissa's condition. Nick couldn't help but be struck by how out of character she seemed. And it was his fault, wasn't it? Had he knocked the compassion right out of her?

"So what did you two kids do while we were away?" Melissa asked, changing the subject.

Nick waited for Stacy to say something, but she only continued to stare at the table.

"We just hung around town and took in the sights," Nick said.

"Ah," Melissa nodded. She looked at Stacy, then looked back at Nick, giving him a questioning look.

"I think I'm going to go back to bed," Stacy suddenly said. "I'm not feeling too good."

She got out of her chair. To Nick's relief, she leaned over and hugged Melissa.

"I'm sorry about your dad. I know how that feels," she said.

"Thanks, kiddo," Melissa said.

Stacy then walked out of the room without saying a word to Jason or Nick. They listened to her walk back upstairs and shut her door. Even Blitz watched her go with a curious expression.

"What the hell happened to her?" Melissa asked shortly after the door shut.

"I've been wondering since we got home if you replaced Stacy with a robot while we were gone," Jason said.

"She even hugged me like one," Melissa added.

Nick didn't know what to say. He leaned back in his chair and sighed.

"You don't have to tell us, Nick," Jason said. "I've got a pretty good idea anyway."

Nick looked at him, only a little surprised.

"You shot her down, didn't you?" Melissa said, comprehension suddenly dawning in her eyes.

For a moment, Nick said nothing. Then he nodded a little.

"God damn it, Nick. The girl's been out of sorts lately anyway, what with the bad dreams and stuff. And now you go and tell her you're too good for her, too?"

He gave her an angry look.

"That's not what this is about," he said.

"I know damn well what it's about, Nick! You're just being the same whiney, mopey bitch you've been since the moment I met you," Melissa said, getting angry herself.

'Aww, I'm so troubled. Oh, I'm too dangerous to be around. I'm being stalked by demons.' Melissa said, waving her arms around mockingly.

Jason put a firm hand on her arm.

"Cool it," he told her.

She sat back and continued to look at Nick disapprovingly.

Jason turned to him.

"Melissa's being over dramatic, but she's right, Nick. We know how you feel about her. Anyone that spent more than five minutes with the two of you would know it. Pushing her away just because you don't want her to get hurt is the most backwards thing you could do. Don't you see you're hurting her more this way?"

Nick stood up quickly and violently, shoving his chair into the wall and making Blitz jump up and run into the other room.

"So what do you want me to do, Jason? Tell her I love her and then watch her get ripped to pieces? Yeah, I have feelings for her. Yeah everybody knows it. Everybody. That damned thing can read my mind. I feel it crawling around in my brain every time I'm close to it. If I don't shove these feelings away, The Whisper is going to use them. And Stacy's going to suffer because of it."

"Either way she suffers, Nick," Jason said to him.

Nick glared at him, but Jason didn't look away. They both knew he was right.

So instead of arguing further, Nick just stormed out of the kitchen and out the front door, grabbing his sword from its spot by the door frame as he went.

"That's his answer to everything, isn't it?" Melissa said. "Run out the door."

Jason sighed.

"He can't run forever. No matter how good at it he is."

10

"Can't run forever," Jason repeated to himself an hour later, kicking a rock out of the dirt and watching it skid into a pile of old wooden beams.

He and Blitz were standing in a construction site - one that the owners of the project had abandoned when the economy went south. No one had bothered to come and take down the skeleton of the building that had never had a chance to see use.

He and Melissa had driven by the place once on their way to pick up Nick after a particularly nasty fight downtown. Jason remembered thinking at the time that the place looked like a sanctuary of sorts. A place to let one's feet and mind wander. He also imagined that most nights this place was full of crack heads and homeless people, but tonight it was eerily quiet. In fact, Jason had noticed a strange dwindling of New Orleans' homeless population and a sudden surge in the number of murdered John Does found lying in pools of blood on the streets.

The Whisper, without a doubt. New Orleans' own demonic Jack the Ripper.

He was taking his life into his hands wandering out here alone. Well…alone except for Blitz. Jason frankly didn't care if he encountered a monster or not, however. He needed a distraction. Any distraction - even a violent one.

Blitz trotted around him in circles, smelling everything at least once. His tail wagged as he looked up at Jason.

"Thanks for the company, furball," Jason said to him.

Blitz panted happily and then went back to sniffing.

"I think you and I are the only ones acting normal these days," he said as the dog trotted off.

Jason laughed a bit. He was the one wearing sunglasses at night and carrying a weighted chain wrapped around his arm and hidden under his sleeve.

Normal, indeed.

And yet with Melissa's internal struggles, Nick's resentment over their judgment of his actions, and Stacy's odd and uncharacteristic sullenness, he did feel that he was the only one acting like himself.

And what did that mean, exactly? What kind of "himself" did Jason really have to be like? Who was he anymore?

Truth was, he wasn't sure. Raven was dead. His revenge was more or less sated. His family was still missing, but he still hadn't received a single lead on their whereabouts. All he knew was that they had not returned to their old apartment in Atlanta and none of the neighbors had heard from them at all since their abduction, a crime no one in the neighborhood bothered to report for fear of Raven.

Jason felt as though he were stagnating. He loved his new life with his friends. He reveled in the new strength he had developed in himself, both physically and mentally. But he really didn't have much of a purpose now. Occasionally someone else's purpose perhaps, but never his own.

"Ah, stop whining," Jason said to himself.

His current situation was just a bridge anyway, one between his past and his future. He would find his family again and have his life back. It was only a matter of time.

He saw Blitz's ears perk up suddenly. The dog was looking down the hill at the far side of the property - the hill overlooking the lakeside dock down below.

Jason walked over to stand beside the dog. A large boat had just anchored below and several men were standing on the dock, roping it off. One of the men was directing a truck that was backing up nearby.

He watched while the men began unloading things from the boat. Large crates. Heavy, from the look of it. A few of the crates were loaded onto the truck.

Another man emerged from the boat and stopped the men carrying one of the crates before it could be loaded. He pulled out a crowbar and began prying the crate open.

"Shit," Jason muttered when he saw the contents of the container.

Guns. Lots and lots of guns. Automatic weapons of large caliber, he thought. He was a ways away, but he could make out well enough what was going on. This was a shipment from an illegal arms deal. Firearm sales of any kind were illegal since the Raven-brokered Peace and Disarmament Act.

"I knew it," he said. "RavenCorp. Probably McElroy's men now that the runt himself is gone."

Of course, it may have just been some random drug smugglers arming their gangs, but Jason didn't think so. Those weapons would have been far too expensive for just any street thugs. No, this had Raven's stench all over it. Many suspected that Raven played such an important part in banning firearms on American soil because he wanted to corner the market himself and bring it underground. Jason thought there was little doubt of the accuracy of that belief now.

The man examining the weapons picked up a large rifle. He set its butt on his shoulder and peered through the scope, first out at the water, then at some of the men, who gave a startled jump when the gun was pointed their way, and then at the construction site.

Jason saw the man tense up soon after pointing the scope in his direction.

He had been seen.

Jason quickly backed up into the shadows behind a beam. Fat lot of good it would do now. He peaked out in time to see the man heading up the hill, alone, with the rifle still in his hands. He barked back an order at the other men to keep working.

Jason let the weighted end of his chain fall to the ground. He thought of running but realized he would rather face the man and get some answers about what he had just witnessed.

"Looks like we're going to get some action after all, Blitz," he whispered to the dog.

Blitz's hackles rose up and a low growl emitted from his throat as the man got closer.

As the man climbed up the hill and closed the distance between them, Jason was struck by an odd sense of familiarity. The way the man walked, the way he carried his weapon, his height and stature.

He shrugged it off and then stepped out from behind the beam as the man made it to the top of the hill.

"Whoever you are, friend, you picked the wrong night to go sightseeing," the man with the gun said.

"Maybe. What is it I'm seeing, exactly?" Jason answered, trying to sound confident but unthreatening in case the man decided he would rather talk than fight.

"None of your business," was the man's reply.

So much for that approach.

Jason took a couple of steps closer to the man. Blitz followed, still growling.

"Back up, man. Trust me, you don't want any of this," the man warned as Jason got closer.

"Depends," Jason said, "on whether or not you work for Jacob Raven."

The man seemed startled, and apparently decided talking would not suffice. To Jason's surprise, however, he threw down his gun before closing the distance between them.

"Now I know I can't let you go," the man said, and took a swing at Jason.

Jason stepped back, avoiding the blow. The man swung again with a vicious left hook. This time Jason blocked the blow with his stronger right arm and returned the man's aggression with a sturdy head-butt.

The man stumbled back a step.

"You're going to pay for that, Dreads," he said, referring to Jason's growing mane of dreadlocks.

Blitz barked anxiously as the two men traded blows. Jason had dropped his chain and resorted to his boxing skills. He didn't want to really hurt this guy. Not if he was going to question him about RavenCorp later. And there was still something bugging him. Something about the way the man moved, the sound of his voice, and the word he had just called him.

Dreads. The man was referring to his hair, but why didn't it feel that way?

Jason kneed the man in the ribs, but that barely slowed him down. This guy was good. He was taller than Jason but not as broad. About the same height as his brother.

Dreads.

Dredd.

Jason gasped and hesitated just long enough for a right hook to hit him square in the jaw.

"Colin?" Jason muttered as he reeled back.

Jason thought he saw the man's eyes widen a bit in the dark.

"I don't care how you know me, kid, but this lesson isn't over,"

Jason had been a good fifty pounds of muscle and several inches of hair shorter the last time his brother saw him. It was no wonder Colin didn't recognize him. He shoved Jason back.

"Colin, it's me…."

The man came forward again, and this time Jason reacted out of instinct. When the man reached out to grab him, Jason grabbed his arms, planted a foot in his midsection, and rolled back, carrying the man up and over him.

Jason heard a crunch as the man flew over him, landing on a pile of plywood and metal behind him.

Jason quickly got to his feet.

"Colin, it's me!" he repeated.

Colin lay on the ground, his chest rising and falling rapidly. Jason couldn't tell in the dark, but perhaps he had knocked the wind out of him.

He walked over and saw with horror that that was not the case.

Sticking about six inches out of Colin's chest was a long, jagged piece of wood. Colin had fallen on top of it, and the thing had gone right through him.

"No!" Jason yelled and fell to his knees beside Colin.

Colin's eyes were wide and confused. His breath was ragged, and a pool of blood was quickly growing around him.

"Jason?" Colin said, and before Jason could reply, Colin laid his head back, took another ragged breath, and then stopped breathing altogether.

Colin Dredd, Jason's older brother and hero since he was four, was dead.

And Jason had killed him.

Nick was perched atop a cement pillar overlooking a cemetery when he heard Blitz's bark in the distance. He had been thinking about Stacy and what Jason and Melissa had said about him being unfair to her. Maybe it was true. Maybe he was wrong to push her away. He was just so damn scared of losing her, of losing all of them really, that he felt that he had to.

He shook off his thoughts and focused on the sound. He didn't know how he knew it was Blitz, but he didn't stop to question.

Then he saw something out of the corner of his eye. A shape moved in the trees on the opposite end of the graveyard. A figure in the shape of a man glided out of the trees towards the source of the sound.

The Dark Man. The Dark Man had been watching him again.

Why would he go after Blitz? And what was Blitz doing out here anyway?

Nick decided he would have to get there first and find out.

Jason had pulled his brother off of the pile of broken wood and was holding him. He was covered in blood and tears. He had been searching for his family for nearly two years now, and now he had found one of them only to watch him die? At his own hand? What cruel trick of fate was this?

Colin had been the one to sell them out. Colin had been the one to take the job with Raven in exchange for his family's freedom. Jason should hate him for that. But instead, all he felt was loss. Throughout all of his childhood, Jason had worshipped his older brother. It was Colin who had decided to shorten their last name to Dredd, and Jason had honored that just because his brother's idea of cool had always been his as well.

Colin the basketball star. Colin the straight-A student. Colin the man who had been more of a father to Jason than his real father ever had.

Dead. In his arms.

"This won't do," a voice said from behind him.

Jason jumped. Blitz yelped in surprise, and then started backing away, making a sound that was half-growl and half terrified whimper.

Jason turned to see a tall man dressed in black standing behind him.

"Hello, Mr. Dredd. I see you've finally found your brother," the man remarked. His cool blue eyes were fixed on Jason and a smug smile was on his face.

"You!" Jason said in anger and recognition, almost hoping the man would give him a reason to get up and kill him for interrupting his mourning.

"Ah, that's right. You've seen me before, haven't you Jason?" The Dark Man commented.

"Raven's mentor. Now, pardon me, but I don't give a flying fuck who you are. My brother is dead." Jason said, suddenly even more ready to kill the interloper.

"Leave him alone!" came a voice from above and to the right of them.

Jason turned to see Nick on top of a beam with his sword in his hand.

"Ah, we have company, Mr. Dredd. The man that seems to be everywhere these days."

"Nick," Jason said, suddenly brought back to the shame of what he had done. "it's Colin. I killed him."

"What?" Nick exclaimed, jumping down and coming to kneel by Jason's side.

"Yes," The Dark Man said. "Mr. Dredd here seems to have murdered his long lost brother. Tragic, really."

Jason roared and jumped to his feet, dropping Colin's body and lunging at The Dark Man. Nick tried to hold him back, but Jason was a good four inches taller and about 75 pounds heavier.

"Don't do it! This guy's dangerous!" Nick called out.

The Dark Man floated back beyond Jason's grasp, laughing a little.

"The Hero's right, Jason. I am dangerous," he said. "but…I didn't come here to hurt you. I came here to help."

"How!!?" Jason yelled. "How can you help me! I just killed my brother!"

"By fixing it, of course."

Jason stopped moving, and Nick looked at The Dark Man incredulously.

"Fixing it?"

"Yes," The Dark Man replied and snapped his fingers.

Suddenly, the sound of coughing erupted from behind Jason and Nick. Jason spun around.

Colin was alive, writhing on the ground and fighting for air.

Jason ran to his side. Nick watched him scoop his brother up. Colin finally gained a breath, looked at Jason, and then looked at The Dark Man.

"No," Nick heard him mutter. "not him."

87

Nick turned back to The Dark Man, and nearly jumped out of his skin to see that the man was standing mere inches from his face now.

"You. Meet me at the barn in the woods near your house. I know you've been there before. I've watched you. I wasn't the only one, you know. I know about the demon. I know how you can stop him."

"Don't listen to him!" Colin yelled hoarsely.

"Do you…know who I am?" Nick asked The Dark Man, ignoring Colin's warning.

"Oh yes, Nick. If I can bring your friend's brother back from the dead, imagine what else I can do for you. Meet me there, and we'll talk."

The Dark Man then took a step back and vanished. It was as if he had simply melted into the darkness. There one second and gone the next.

Nick stared into the empty night for a moment and then turned back to Jason and his injured brother.

But Colin was not injured. As Nick got closer, he could see that Colin was covered in blood…but no wounds.

"How?" Jason asked, seeming more shocked than any of them.

"The man is evil," Colin said. "Raven's advisor. I thought that bastard had abandoned him after the bounty hunters showed up. Raven sure wouldn't shut up about it."

"Raven…," Jason said, narrowing his eyes. "He's still alive?"

Colin chuckled. "The sorcerer brought me back from the dead, didn't he?"

Jason looked up at Nick, and Nick couldn't help but plop down on the dirt beside them. This night was becoming far too weird for either of them.

Colin brushed Jason's hand off and stood up. He took off his bloody shirt and tossed it aside. Then Nick and Jason watched as he walked over to the rifle he had dropped earlier and picked it up.

Nick wondered for a moment if the man meant to use the weapon against them, but instead he began walking towards the hill nearby. Jason and Nick followed and watched as Colin hurled the weapon into the lake below.

Nick noticed some men packing up a truck. At the sound of the splash, they scattered aboard the truck and sped off. Raven's men. So that was why Jason was out here.

"I'm done with this," Colin said as he walked back to them. "First you and Mom get kidnapped, then I have to take orders from a goddamn warlock, and now there're guys with razor whips wandering around the building. I'm done with Raven. He can come after me if he wants, but this ends tonight."

"Colin," Jason said softly, his voice still wavering from the shock. "I…I killed you."

Colin walked over to his brother and placed a hand upon his shoulder.

"You're not a killer, Jason. You may have made yourself look like one now, but I can still see it in your eyes. You were always the best of us."

Jason placed his hand over Colin's. Nick and Blitz stood back and watched the exchange between the two.

"How is Mom doing?" Colin asked.

Jason's face darkened in confusion.

"I…I don't know. I've been looking for her."

Colin took a step back in surprise.

"But…Raven told me when he sent me overseas that he had let you both go."

Jason shook his head slowly.

"No, Colin. He kept me for months, away from the others. I only got out because some friends sprung me," Jason said, pointing a thumb back at Nick. "and then I got caught again. Raven kept me in a cell for more than half a year that time. That's how I got like this, Colin. He changed me. He tore my soul out. There's no telling what he did to Mom, if she's even still alive."

Colin sat down on the dirt and put his face in his hands.

"I should have known that little fuck was lying."

"It's what he does best," Jason said. "I tried to kill him once, but obviously it didn't take."

Colin looked up at him. "That was you? I heard about the raid at the chicken factory. And I knew you were involved," Colin said, nodding at Nick. "but I had no idea my baby brother had anything to do with it."

"Raven threw himself off the roof," Nick said. "Despite what he says, your brother would have saved him, not killed him."

Jason gave Nick a disapproving look.

But Colin nodded. "Yeah. That sounds about right. Your heart was always bigger than your fists, Jason. Well…metaphorically speaking these days."

Colin stood up and looked his brother up and down.

"Damn, you've been eating your Wheaties."

Jason chuckled a bit.

"Bet I could beat you at basketball now."

"Shit, son. You still wouldn't have a prayer."

Nick watched the two of them together. It was obvious that they were brothers. Even with Jason in his changed state, the resemblance was there. Colin was taller, but slimmer now. He was built like a soldier, lean and toned. His hair was short and clean-cut, in direct contrast to Jason's dreads, which had become quite long. His skin was a slight shade lighter than Jason's. He seemed to carry himself with confidence, even in lieu of the current circumstances. He was quite a striking figure, and Nick could see why Jason had looked up to him.

"So you and The Hero roll together?" Colin asked.

Jason looked at Nick again.

"Hah. We don't call him that around the house, but yeah, Nick's my friend."

"Nick," Colin said, walking over to Nick. "you've been making a lot of enemies, man."

"You don't know the half of it," Nick replied.

"You'd be surprised," Colin said. "All I can tell you is that you need to watch your back. That asshole in the cloak talks about you all the damn time. And now Raven's got some European bad asses gunning for you."

Jason and Nick exchanged a look. Great. All they needed were more enemies.

"You should come with us, Colin," Nick said.

"Yeah," Jason agreed. "together we can look for Mom."

Colin looked at the ground for a moment and then began pacing back and forth, rubbing the back of his neck. Finally, he shook his head.

"No. You're safer if I'm somewhere else. So is Mom. Raven doesn't take kindly to deserters. Right now, he's just watching you guys, but if I'm with you…"

"We've handled him before," Nick said.

"And I wouldn't mind another excuse to go after his ass," Jason said.

But Colin just shook his head again.

"Sorry bro, but I…I just died, you know?" Colin looked up at the sky, his eyes reflecting in the moonlight. "I should still be dead. Black magic can't be good for the soul. Neither can betraying my family."

Jason looked defeated but let his brother have his say.

"I need some time to figure things out. I've been a thug for too long. Hell, any time at all was too long. I turned my back on everyone who needed me. I let you and Mom rot in a cell while that asshole Raven cut me checks. I…I hurt people while I was working for him, Jason. Hell, I even killed people. None of 'em were saints, but that's blood I never wanted on my hands."

Now Jason shook his head.

"Colin, I've been without my family for two years. Half of that I was alone in a cell. Don't walk away from me again. I need you."

Colin looked heartbroken. He walked over to Jason and wrapped his arms around him.

"You aint losing me this time, baby bro. I aint dead and I aint turning my back on you. I love you. You know that."

He stepped back and looked at his younger brother.

"I know you'll find Mom. And you can tell her I love her when you do. I'm just…not ready to face her yet. Not after what I did. Not after all that's happened."

Jason nodded, and Nick saw the moonlight hit a tear as it fell from Jason's downcast head.

"Then come back to me, Colin. When you're back on your feet."

Colin smiled and waved. "Will do, baby bro."

He looked at Nick now. "Take care of him, okay? He may be big as hell now, but inside he's still the same little kid I used to make fun of for watching the Discovery Channel."

Nick smiled. "I will, I promise."

Colin smiled back and walked away. After a few steps, he turned back, as if he had thought of something.

"Don't trust a word the sorcerer says. The man's pure evil, I can tell you that. I may owe him my life, but I never want to see that creepy piece of shit again."

"Who is he, Colin?" Nick called after him.

"I don't know," Colin replied. "Nobody does."

Colin started walking away again. Nick made his way over to Jason. He put a hand on Jason's shoulder and they watched his brother leave.

Suddenly, Colin stopped again and turned around.

"I just remembered something. I don't know if it'll help or not. The sorcerer…"

Colin was shouting now, and his words echoed across the construction site.

"…his name's David."

11

"David," Melissa said, interrupting Nick mid-sentence. "His name is David, isn't it?"

Nick and Jason watched her bring her legs up to her chest and wrap her arms around them. There was a numb, distant look in her eyes - the look of someone who was accepting something uncomfortable.

"Melissa, it couldn't be your uncle. The odds of that are…" Jason said, trailing off. He knew better than to inject too much logic into their lives. If the sorcerer was Melissa's sadistic uncle, the coincidence would be par for the course. Nothing about their lives made sense. Nothing played into reason. The supernatural had become commonplace. He and Nick had just witnessed a man vanish into thin air after resurrecting someone, and Nick had told them he had seen the man fly on previous occasions.

"It could, and I think it is," she said. "Nick said his eyes changed color. The last day I saw my uncle…the last day he and his friends hurt me…I saw his eyes change. One turned green and the other black. I saw it happen right in front of my eyes. One minute they were blue, then they seemed to turn red and then, all of a sudden, they were a new color entirely."

"Maybe it's just someone who can do the same things your uncle could," Nick said, fearing Melissa was right.

Melissa shook her head. "With salt-and-pepper black hair? About six feet tall? A black beard? With the same name? Come on, Nick."

Nick sighed and sat back, unable to argue with the logic. Jason gripped the armrests of the chair he was sitting in.

"That would also explain why the asshole never appeared when I was with Raven. He was avoiding me. Hell, he might have even had a hand in getting me hired in the first place," Melissa continued.

"Yeah, probably. I knew it didn't make sense that you had worked for Raven that long and never saw the guy. So if it is him…if it is your uncle, then we know what we have to do," Jason said.

Nick immediately shook his head.

"The man's trouble, and I get the feeling he's very powerful. If we confront him, we'll be charging in blindly to something that could kill us. We don't know what he's capable of. It's best I go alone. See what he knows and ask him if he really is your uncle, Melissa."

"No," Melissa said sternly. "Nick, there's no way in hell I'm letting you walk out that door without me."

"Or me," Jason added.

"Or me," came a voice from the stairs. They all looked up to see Stacy standing there. She looked grim and pale. She had also been losing weight over the past few weeks, and it had never been more apparent.

"Stacy, if you've heard our story, you know that this guy isn't normal. He's not like those punks we beat up in the warehouse or one of Raven's usual goons. He could kill us, and the last thing we need is…."

"Don't you dare say it, Nick," Stacy interrupted angrily. "Don't you dare say that the last thing you need is me holding you back. Don't say I'm dead weight. I'm just as good as any of you. You may all be good in a fight, but I can shoot any one of you between the eyes before you get within ten feet of me. So don't you dare say you don't need me."

Melissa looked at Jason and shot him a surprised and amused expression.

"You're right, Stacy. We do need you," she said.

Nick looked at her disapprovingly.

"I'm calling the shots on this one, and I say we'll need her," Melissa said to him.

"But he wants to see me," he said.

Melissa got to her feet and stared Nick dead in the eyes.

"And he cut into my flesh once a week for a year! He scarred my body and he killed any trace of the little girl I used to be, Nick! All this anger I have is because of him! This is my show and my fight! If you've got a problem with it, you can stay behind!"

Nick looked up at her for a moment, and then slowly shook his head.

"Fine," he said simply.

Stacy went back upstairs to grab her crossbow and Melissa went to her room to change. Jason took hold of Nick's arm.

"Don't worry. We'll play nice until we have our answers, but then we have to let Melissa do what she has to do. I've already watched her put part of her past behind her. Now it's time to put the rest of it in its grave. As her friends, we owe that to her."

Nick stood up, still looking uneasy.

"I know. And I won't lie and say that I don't get the feeling this guy deserves to get his ass kicked anyway. It's just...he knows things about me. And if someone like that knows more about me than I do...what does that say about me?"

Jason put his shades back on. Melissa and Stacy came clumping down the stairs. He turned to Nick.

"Let's go and find out."

Nick led the way through the woods with the others close behind him. Blitz kept pace, but he knew that the dog would likely take off as soon as they found The Dark Man. Nick had noticed that the dog was afraid of the sorcerer the same way he was afraid of The Whisper. When either came near, the dog would cower and hide.

Nick wondered if they shouldn't be cowering as well.

As the edge of the clearing came into view, Melissa pulled Stacy aside and said something quietly to her. Stacy nodded and then headed off, circling around the clearing to the east. Nick silently approved. Not only could Stacy watch their backs with her crossbow trained on David's face, but she would, hopefully, be out of harm's way as well.

Melissa gripped her staff tightly, and then looked at Jason and Nick in turn. She nodded and then led the way into the clearing.

David was waiting for them, sitting cross-legged on the roof of the barn, looking smug, comfortable, and not the least bit surprised that Nick had brought friends.

"Hello again, niece."

The three of them paused at the edge of the clearing. The barn was huge, old, and decrepit, looking as if it would fall to pieces at any moment. Nick had discovered the abandoned building several months ago while exploring. He could not have imagined that the next time he saw the place would be under these conditions.

"Hello, you child-raping mother fucker," Melissa replied.

David stood up and crossed his arms in front of his chest.

"Come now, I never violated you in that way."

"You might as well have. I've still got scars for every time you cut me. And I'm about to give you ten for every damn one you gave me."

David shrugged.

"It was nothing personal, Melissa. You were just a tool. A key to a doorway I was trying to open. I suppose I owe you a debt of gratitude, really. Without you, and my idiot brother who let me use you, I would not be the man I am today."

"Is that really what you are," Jason asked. "a man? Because you look more like a monster."

David laughed.

"Aren't we all, Jason? Aren't you a monster for letting Raven turn you into the hollowed-out shell of a man you are now? Isn't Melissa a monster for letting Bart and I turn her into a vessel of rage and violence? And as for the other two of you here today…oh, the stories I could tell."

So he knew about Stacy. So much for that advantage. As long as she kept him in her sights, it didn't matter if she were hidden or not.

Nick suddenly thought to look for Blitz. The dog had already booked it. So much the better. One less friend to worry about. He turned back to David.

"I believe you promised to tell me exactly what kind of monster you think I am," Nick said.

David sighed and shook his head.

"Oh Nick, that deal only applied if you trusted me and came alone. You didn't, so…that knowledge is forfeit."

"No," Nick said, shaking his head. "I'm not walking out of here until you tell me who I am."

"Who you are isn't a terribly interesting story. What you are, on the other hand…."

"Quit playing games, David. If you know something Nick doesn't, spill it while you still have teeth," Melissa said.

"Oh I know a lot of things Nick doesn't. I know he's not what he thinks he is. I know he's capable of things far more important than flipping between rooftops and swinging a sword at muggers."

"Like what?" Nick asked, desperate to gain any information he could out of the man before things turned sour.

"Think about it, Nick. You arrogantly let them call you 'The Hero,' but what kind of hero cuts people up with a sword? What kind of hero wears a mask and stalks in the shadows? You have more in common with that metal beast that follows you than you do with a real hero."

Nick's heart sank a little.

"So you're saying I'm meant to be something else? That I only have these skills to…hurt people?"

"Much more than that, Nick. You can change the world. You were meant to. I can help you do that in the way you truly want to."

"You don't know him at all," Jason said. "Nick doesn't want to hurt people. He is a hero, and you can't make us believe that's not what he's meant to be."

"Why can't I remember what happened to me?" Nick asked.

David seemed to pause for a moment.

"I've been trying to figure that out myself, to be honest. None of the others ever had that problem, as far as I know."

"Others?" Nick said with alarm. "Other what?"

David ignored the question.

"I think…this is just another sign that you're different from the ones that came before. The memory loss, the confusion over what you're supposed to do, the strange emptiness of your aura…plus the physical feats you're capable of…all of these things have lead me to believe that not only are you different from the ones that have come before, you're also better."

Jason could see Melissa getting antsy. He put a hand on her shoulder. They all needed to hear the sorcerer out.

David seemed to study them for a moment.

"Odd," he said. "Speaking of your aura…it looks like the ties between you are a lot…older than I imagined they would be. Especially…."

Suddenly his eyes, now yellow, widened and he burst out into a loud and terrifying laugh.

"That sneaky, selfish bastard. I should have known. Well, Nick, it seems there's even more that you really have no idea about. And the demon must have….oh yes. It's all becoming so clear now."

David nodded, seeming pleased with himself.

"Mystery solved. Turns out you're not so much of an enigma after all, Hero."

"Tell me," Nick said, obviously unamused.

David shook his head.

"No. That little epiphany helped me decide what I'm going to do with you - because I see now that you're not better than the others after all. No. You, my friend, are an accident - an abortion ripped from the womb before your time by that monster's metal fingers."

Nick drew his sword.

"Tell me who I am!" he screamed.

David laughed and shook his head.

"No. I could have helped you. I could have made you worth something, instead of the failure that you are. But you blew that chance when you chose not to trust me, Nick. I've said all I'm going to say. It's time to speak with actions, rather than words."

"You won't touch him, David. You had your little pow-wow. Now, this is between you and me. It's time I paid you back for all the pain you caused me," Melissa said, stepping in front of Nick.

"Have it your way," David said. "I'll have fun killing you both."

The sorcerer shot his hand forward, and Nick and Melissa heard Jason yell in surprise behind them. They turned to see their friend fighting off what seemed to be his own weapon.

"What the hell did you do?" Jason cried. The weighted end of his chain had uncoiled itself from his arm and was reared up in front of him like a snake. It snapped forward twice, nearly clipping him in the head. It took all of Jason's considerable effort to keep the thing from slamming into his own face.

Nick stepped forward to help him, but Jason yelled at him to stop.

"Stay back! I've got this. Now both of you do what you came to do!"

Something whizzed through the air as they turned back to David. The sorcerer casually held up his left hand, and a crossbow bolt stopped in midair just inches from his face.

He snapped his fingers, and the piece of wood broke in two and fell to the ground far below. He then looked in the direction the shot had come from and muttered something.

"Dust," he said.

They heard another twang from the crossbow string. But there was no second shot. Instead, they heard a cry of frustration from the trees.

"That's enough," Melissa said. "No more magic tricks."

She and Nick ran forward, brandishing their weapons.

David grinned. Suddenly, his eyes were not yellow, nor blue, nor green. They were burning red. He lifted his arms to his sides and laughed as a sheet of flame seemed to envelop him. His feet left the ground and he hovered into the air.

"You have no idea what I can do to you," he said. He gestured towards Nick.

Nick felt the ground rumble beneath his running feet. An instant later, large rocks began to erupt from the ground in front of him and around him. He dodged them but had to slow down his approach.

Melissa didn't falter. Her eyes were locked on David. Flying or not, she meant to take him down.

Jason continued to struggle with his now animate chain. He held it away from him in his right hand while trying to grab hold of the "head" with his left. The thing was nearly as strong as he was.

David turned his attention to Melissa.

"Did I leave you a few scars? Poor little girl. Are you ready for a few more?"

He wound his right arm back, and a globe of fire emerged in his hand. He threw the fire like a baseball towards her.

Melissa grunted and tried to jump out of the way. The fireball hit the ground by her foot and exploded, bathing her in a wave of searing flame.

She screamed and rolled to her left, letting the ground extinguish the flames that had caught hold of her hair and her clothes. She then got back to her feet and kept moving forward.

Jason's weapon had redoubled its attack. The other end of the chain now emerged from Jason's sleeve and whipped around him, wrapping him up and simultaneously pulling him back. He fell to the ground as the chain pulled him across the dirt. He felt his back hit something. A tree. The weapon began to wrap itself tightly around the tree and around his neck. His hand pushed the cold steel away from his throat, but he didn't think he would be able to stop the weapon for long. If Melissa and Nick didn't get to David, he would soon be strangled by his own chain.

Stacy ran out of the woods, screaming. She threw a rock at David. It dissolved into nothing as it hit the sheath of flame surrounding him. The sorcerer completely ignored her.

Nick jumped, dodged, and flipped around the rocks erupting from the ground at increasing frequency. He was making little progress towards David. He batted a rock away with his sword, yelling in frustration. He felt something large moving beneath his feet, and before he could move, a boulder the size of his head shot from the ground and clipped him in the chin. Nick's head snapped back. He stumbled a few more steps and then collapsed to the ground unconscious.

"Well, that was depressingly easy," David said, turning his attention away from Nick. He locked eyes with Melissa, who was now almost at the foot of the barn.

"Just you and me now, little girl."

David began to slowly descend through the air towards her. He brought his hands forward, and a wall of fire burst from them in her direction.

It hit her full force. She screamed in pain - but she did not stop.

"Hmph," David said and then hit her again.

This time Melissa didn't even cry out. She braced her arms in front of her face and charged through the flames.

David hit her again, and again, and then yet another time. She was closing the distance between them, and as she did so, his smoldering red eyes were getting wider and wider with alarm.

"Why…won't…you…DIE!!!"

Melissa screamed, and as the last wall of fire hit her, she dropped her staff and launched herself into the air. David attempted to pause in mid-flight, but there was not enough time. Melissa hit him with the force of a linebacker.

The two of them fell the remaining five feet to the ground, David landing on his back and Melissa landing on top of him. Her hair was smoking, her skin was blistered, and her clothes were in ruins, but she seemed only to care about taking her uncle down. Immediately after they hit the ground, she punched him as hard as she could.

The red faded from his eyes. The fire vanished. One of his teeth flew across the grass. Melissa thrust a knee hard into his ribs.

Stacy heard the snap of bone. Jason's chain fell limp around him.

Melissa began to beat him like a rag doll. Jason thought her misguided attack on Nick had been fierce. It was nothing compared to this.

Again and again her fist hit his face. Every time the man attempted to raise his head from the ground, Melissa's knuckles would send it crashing back down again. More teeth flew. A second snap sounded out, and then a third one. The first was his nose. The second was his skull actually cracking.

Jason and Stacy watched in awe as years and years of built-up anger and pain erupted from her fists all over David's face. If the sorcerer's head had been a steel wall, Jason believed she would have hammered right through it.

Just when they believed the man had to be dead from the force of the beating, he managed to bring his hands to Melissa's sides. His fingers stretched wide, and all of a sudden Melissa was sailing through the air away from him.

She landed a good thirty feet away from David, slamming into the ground roughly. Jason pulled free from his chain and crawled to her side. She grimaced and sat up.

They looked up to see David taking to the air again, this time grabbing Nick and swooping with the unconscious boy in tow to the rooftop of the barn.

"No!" Stacy yelled. But there was nothing she could do. All of her ammunition had been turned to dust.

"You weak little shits!" David slurred, blood dripping from his busted lips. One of his eyes was bruised shut and probably damaged beyond repair. The other, now its original blue, glared at them hatefully.

"I don't care what you are! I don't care what you can do because of this little prick! You're still not better than me! I'm the most powerful man alive!"

David looked down at Nick hungrily.

"And when I kill this little failure, I'll be even stronger."

David got to his knees. He reached inside of his cloak and pulled forth a large, wicked knife.

"No!" Stacy screamed again. Melissa and Jason jumped to their feet, but they knew there was nothing either of them could do in time.

David brought the knife into the air, gripping it in both hands.

"You may have been born the way you were, Hero, but I made myself this way out of sheer will. That makes me stronger, and now I'm going to prove it. Now...let me see you the way you really are one last time before I cut your filthy heart out."

For an instant, something amazing happened. All of them saw a flash of something. Energy flowing between them. Each of them glowed for that split second, as if from radiation - none of them stronger than David. They couldn't see Nick, but David's light was less a light and more an absence of one - a black and red wound in the fabric of the air around him.

David stared at Nick, holding the knife high. His mouth bore a bloody grin.

But then he paused. The excitement faded from his eyes and his arms drooped a little.

"Wait...you're not the...."

And then, in the blink of an eye, Melissa saw another light whip past behind her uncle. This one a reflection of sunlight off of metal.

David's eyes grew wide and he jerked forward slightly. His arms wavered, and then went limp, dropping the knife harmlessly beside Nick's head. David slowly turned to look behind him. Melissa, Jason and Stacy could see blood coursing from a fresh, deep wound on his back.

But that was not all they saw.

Standing behind David was a familiar, six-and-a-half-foot tall metal figure.

David looked at The Whisper in surprise.

"You...you know too, don't you?" he said weakly.

The Whisper leaned forward, bringing his flaming eyes close to David's battered face.

"*Mine,*" they all heard the demon say in a raspy voice.

And then his bladed hand swiped through the air again, and the next thing Melissa saw was her uncle's head sailing through the air towards her. It landed with a thud, rolling to a stop near her feet. His blue eye seemed to look up at her, an expression of shock and dismay on what was left of his face.

They all stared at the head for a moment, and when they looked back up, The Whisper was gone.

A few minutes later, they had Nick back on the ground, returning to consciousness. Jason had boosted Stacy to the edge of the roof, and she had climbed the rest of the way, handing Nick down to them. Blitz trotted out of the woods to meet them, content now that the evil of The Dark Man and The Whisper were gone - one gone forever.

While the others tended to Nick, Melissa stood over David's severed head. She replayed in her mind every hurt he had ever inflicted upon her. Every cut. Every bruise. Every invasive touch or intimidating remark. Every scar she would carry with her forever.

Jason and Stacy looked up at her. They did not say a word. They knew that now was Melissa's moment to say goodbye to the pain of her past. Her tormentor. Her own version of The Whisper or Jacob Raven was gone now. She had defeated her personal boogie man since childhood. She hadn't killed him, but she had defeated him just the same.

"Goodbye, David," she said. "I hope you're rotting in Hell already."

The others watched as she took a few steps back. They weren't certain what she was going to do at first, but then it became alarmingly apparent.

Melissa skipped forward and punted David's head like a soccer ball all the way across the clearing and into the trees. They heard it crash through the bushes and leaves, coming to a rest where birds, squirrels and worms would devour it over the course of days. A fitting end, they all thought.

Melissa looked in the direction of her uncle's head for a moment and then turned to them, her face charred but beaming.

They smiled back. There were no words for a moment like this. The end of one road and the beginning of another.

12

Six hundred miles away, Patricia Rolanos sat bolt upright in her bed. She had been seconds from falling asleep, and then something had lit up the inside of her eyelids like Christmas lights.

Had she fallen asleep? Was that another dream? What exactly was it she saw?

She took a deep breath, ran a hand through her short blonde hair, and focused on the image still fresh in her mind.

Lights. Strands of light - strings might actually be a better word - running between shapes. People? Lights running between people?

A black and red mass looming over someone, with other lights of other colors nearby. She didn't know why, but seeing that red light made her panic. Her heart had nearly leaped out of her throat when the lights appeared.

"What the hell was that?" she asked the empty apartment.

Patricia rubbed her eyes, deciding to forget the vision and try to return to her afternoon nap. It was all she had to look forward to these days. Her mornings were spent working a crappy temp job and her evenings were spent looking for better employment before returning home to care for her comatose brother, Benjamin. She talked to Kurt once or twice a week, but she hadn't heard from Nick in over a month. Maybe it was time to call him. Whenever Patricia needed an encouraging word about the seemingly directionless state of her life, Nick was the one to call.

Patricia opened her eyes and flopped back on the bed.

And then her blood turned to ice in her veins.

When she had lain down just then, she thought she had seen something out of the corner of her eye.

Patricia turned her head to the right and screamed.

Benjamin was standing in the corner of her apartment. He was standing slightly in the shadows between the window and the wall, partly hidden in the shadows.

He was wearing the same button-up shirt tucked into brown slacks that she had dressed him in that morning. This wasn't a dream, and yet…it had to be, didn't it?

He stared at her with his mouth slightly open.

"Ben? Oh my god, Ben, are you alright?" Patricia sat up, yanking her covers down and moving towards him

Benjamin didn't answer, but Patricia noticed something. His lips weren't just apart, they were moving slightly. Slowly and purposefully. As if he were trying to speak but no sound was coming out.

She calmed down a little, knowing it was ridiculous to be afraid of her ten-year-old brother, but somehow she was. There was something unnatural about Ben's appearance, aside from the fact that he was awake and standing in her bedroom.

There was something slightly…faded about him. When she reached him, her fears were confirmed. She reached out for her brother and her hand coasted right through him as if through smoke.

The Benjamin she saw before her was not made of flesh and blood. She turned from him and ran down the hall, throwing open the door to her brother's room. Sure enough, he was still there, lying in his bed wearing those same clothes.

Patricia slowly returned to the room and sat down on the bed in front of the apparition.

"What do you want, Ben?" she asked, calmer this time, uncertain if this was truly her brother or simply a figment of her own damaged mind.

The boy took a step forward, and Patricia gasped. When he stepped forward, it was in slow motion. He moved like a child moving through water.

She also noticed that the light shining through the bedroom curtains shone through him, as though he were slightly translucent.

"Ben, is that really you?"

The boy reached the edge of the bed. His hand slowly rose in front of him, reaching for her. His lips continued to move soundlessly.

"Get away!" she screamed, suddenly terrified again. She grabbed a pillow and hurled it towards him.

The pillow sailed through the boy as if through a hologram, but the boy reacted. His arm rose, at normal speed, to block the projectile.

She heard a startled cry come from his previously silent lips. He then dissipated like a cloud of smoke before the pillow even hit the floor.

She sat there, breathing heavily and feeling waves of panic wash over her.

Patricia stared at the spot where the apparition had stood seconds before, her mind racing through the possibilities of what she could have just witnessed.

Was it a hallucination? Or had Benjamin really been trying to reach out to her somehow?

If it was her brother, what was he trying to tell her? As she thought about it, she realized that she had little doubt that this theory was true. Benjamin had been trying to tell her something - trying hard to communicate despite his unspeaking lips and his hindered motion. It was only when she threw the pillow that his voice actually became audible.

She scooted back, sitting against the headboard, eyes locked on the edge of her mattress. She kept telling herself that her brother had meant her no harm.

Patricia sat there for almost an hour before falling back asleep.

She dreamed of lights, like strands of Christmas decorations, wrapped around people she loved.

Nick lay in his own bed late that evening, nursing a slight headache but otherwise fine. He was happy to see Melissa put an old ghost to rest and was still pleased that Jason had found his brother again, but David's words haunted him. In fact, he felt more lost at that moment than he had since the beginning.

"Knock knock," came a voice from the doorway.

Nick looked over to see Stacy standing there. She was leaning against the door frame with one arm stretched above her. Her head lay against the crook of her elbow and a small smile played across her lips. What got Nick's heart racing was what she was wearing - or rather, what she wasn't. Stacy stood there wearing nothing but a skimpy t-shirt and a pair of cotton underwear.

"Hey. Didn't know you were still up," Nick said, trying not to stare.

Stacy entered the room.

"I haven't been sleeping so well lately. I'm sure you've heard that through the rumor mill by now."

Without asking, Stacy pushed Nick's covers aside and crawled into bed with him. She immediately pressed herself against him. She lay on her side while he lay on his back, and her hand settled on his chest. Nick could feel the swell of her breast against his arm. Somehow he knew that she was well aware of that.

"Thinking about today?" she asked.

"Yeah. Can't get what David said out of my head," he replied.

Stacy nodded. Her hand traced invisible circles on his chest. He could feel goosebumps rise on his skin.

"You shouldn't take anything that man said to heart. Whatever he was, he was powerful. But I also think he was bat-shit crazy."

Nick smirked briefly, but he wasn't really sure if the state of David's sanity invalidated the truth of his words.

"He said I was…meant for something else, Stace. Something he seemed to think was a darker path than the one I'm taking."

She brought her hand up from his chin and placed it upon Nick's cheek.

"I don't care what he said, Nick. And I don't care what you are or aren't meant for. You're the most compassionate and beautiful person I've ever met, and nothing anyone says can change that."

For that moment, with her looking into his eyes to drive her point home, Nick didn't see any of the weirdness Stacy had been displaying over the past few weeks. None of the poutiness was there. None of the sullenness was there. None of the quiet, simmering anger was there. There was only Stacy, giving him the same heartfelt affection he had come to love from her.

He wished he could kiss her then. The bare skin and the sultry warmth of her body helped, but it was her eyes that called to him - that made him want her in a way far deeper than physical intimacy.

But then something came back into her eyes. Something strangely foreign. Her lips formed a hungry grin. Before Nick knew it, she wrapped her leg around him and was straddling his lap.

"St…" Nick started, but was startled into silence when Stacy began kissing his neck.

"I…need you to know…how important you are to me, Nick…" she whispered in between kisses.

"Stacy...please," Nick protested, but couldn't help but close his eyes and almost lose himself in the pleasure of feeling her lips on his skin and her body laying over his.

"I almost lost you again today..." she continued, "That made me realize how much I need you. How much I want you to need me."

She sat back up and took his hands in hers. She placed them upon her knees, and then slowly traced his palms over her bare legs.

"There's never been anyone that's made me felt more alive than you do," she said. He could hear a small waver in her voice. He knew a part of her was pleading with him.

His hands reached her hips, and then her waist, and still, inch by inch, she brought them higher on her body.

"I don't want to lie to myself any more. I don't want to be protected anymore, Nick. I want you to have me."

His hands trailed up her rib cage. His heart raced and butterflies whirled in his stomach. His mind was a tempest of conflict. How he wanted to keep touching her.

His breath caught in his throat as he felt the undersides of Stacy's bare breasts against his palms.

"I want you to show me I'm worth something to you."

Before she could bring his hands to their destination, Nick yanked them away from her. He picked her up and tossed her off of him onto the mattress and then got up and walked away.

He stood with his back to her for several seconds, catching his breath and running his hands through his hair. Finally, he turned, and she could see the pained expression on his face.

"I told you...I told you that I couldn't," he said. "And even if I could...I don't want it like this."

Stacy lay there, propped up on her arms. Her face at first wore a mask of surprise. She seemed as startled by the situation as he did. But then he saw the sadness enter her eyes. Her cheeks bunched up and her eyes watered. She looked as though he had just told her he hated her.

Then that sadness...very quickly...turned to anger. She looked at him with eyes that seemed to burn.

"So it's true then," she said softly. "I'm really not good enough for you."

He reached out for her, stung by those words.

"Stacy, you know that's not what I mean."

She got up and walked over to the doorway. She paused when she got there, her back still to him.

"One day you're going to die out there, Nick. And when you do, you'll be alone. You'll have no one to blame but yourself. You know that, don't you?"

Then she left him there. He stood against the wall for a moment, her words echoing inside his head.

Yeah, Nick thought as he sunk to the floor, feeling crushed and hopeless.

Yeah, he did know that.

13

The next few days were blissfully uneventful. Nick didn't know if he could take anymore action or drama. The four of them spent lazy afternoons laughing, watching TV, going out to eat, and in Melissa and Stacy's case, going to and from work. Jason even picked up a job as a part-time cook in the diner they worked at.

Nick spent most of his time doing his usual thing: roaming the woods between their house and the city and walking the streets of New Orleans without his mask and sword during the day - and with them when night fell. He tried not to think about Stacy. He tried to focus on the good parts of the last few weeks.

Melissa had taken huge steps forward by confronting her father and her uncle, as well as by coming clean with the rest of them about her past.

Jason had found his older brother again. Sure he had seen him die and be resurrected in front of him, but that strange reunion was still a blessing, as well as one less thing the tortured man had to dwell on.

But Stacy had no such triumph. For too many days and nights, she seemed only to be falling deeper and deeper into depression and anger. She spoke to them very little. She would not make eye contact with Nick at all anymore. None of them knew exactly what was wrong. Melissa still blamed Stacy's dreams, but even she seemed uncertain. Nick couldn't get over Stacy's actions the other night when she had tried to seduce him. She had pleaded with him to take her. The desperation in her voice had frightened him. It was as if she thought the act of physical release could save her from something. He only wished he knew what.

So he distracted himself, looking for trouble or just immersing himself in the ebb and flow of city life.

Dusk was falling, and after a night of aimless wandering, Nick decided to take his favorite shortcut back home. The freeway.

He hopped off of an overpass, landing on the top of a station wagon. His sword was strapped to his back and he was wearing his mask. He didn't want to be seen traffic surfing as Just-Plain-Nick - not that it really mattered. He had no legal identity or public life either way. Still, keeping those icons present was important to him.

His unconventional chariot speeding about at sixty five an hour, Nick began plotting his course - which cars he would hop to next in his journey to the 510 exit. He spotted two large sixteen-wheelers several lanes away. He always tried to ride out the majority of the trip atop the largest truck he could find. Less likely to be noticed that way.

He squinted. He saw something on top of the truck already. It looked like...a person?

Sure enough, Nick saw an arm flail about and heard a small yell from atop the truck. Someone must have climbed on top of it during a stop and gotten stranded.

Nick immediately made his way towards the truck, from the station wagon to a sports car to a pickup truck, eventually leaping to the edge of the sixteen-wheeler, pulling himself to the top.

There was a woman laying there. She was holding on to the surface for dear life. She was Asian, with a small build and muscular arms, wearing a skin-tight black outfit and some kind of black make-up on her face.

Nick quickly approached her with his hand outstretched.

"Give me your hand! I'll get you off this thing!" he yelled over the wind threatening to whip them both off the truck.

"Thank you!" she shouted back, reaching for him.

Yet when Nick reached her, she pulled her hand away and smiled.

"Sucker," she said.

The woman spun her legs around, vaulting her upper body onto her hands. Nick instinctively flipped backwards and landed with his hand on his weapon.

When he looked up, the woman was already on her feet. Behind her, two more people climbed from the cab to the top of the truck. One was an enormous man with a red bandanna and a holstered shotgun. The other was a much smaller man with long black hair, wearing ripped and tattered clothes. A strange whip dangled from his belt.

God, Nick thought. Did the parade of weirdos wanting to hurt him ever end?

"I don't know who you are or who you work for, but if you don't leave me alone, I won't hesitate to make you," Nick warned them. Truth was, he figured he knew who they worked for. These must be the European "bad-asses" Colin had warned them about.

The woman looked at the larger man. They both let out a small laugh.

"Good," the large man said. "I want to see you try. Priesty, give Mr. Hero here something to think about."

Nick barely had time to move his eyes away from the big man before the smaller man moved forward, his arm whipping from his side towards Nick.

He was vaguely aware of something sailing towards his face and moved back an instant before a long metal barb would have raked his eye from his socket.

Nick drew his sword, backing up a few steps, alarmed not only at the apparent ferocity of these three, but also at the fact that they seemed just as at home on the top of a speeding truck as he did. These were no average thugs.

"Who are you?" he asked.

"I'm Brick. This is Bitch and Razorpriest," the big man said, "And you, my friend, are dead."

Jason was flipping pancakes when he heard the commotion behind him. A group of customers were huddling on the other side of the counter, their necks craned up to look at the television mounted on the wall. He could see Melissa on the other side of the diner, her pace slowing as she caught sight of the TV as well.

He stepped away from the sizzle of the grill long enough to hear what was being broadcast.

"To those of you just joining us, the situation is this: A traffic copter making a routine patrol of interstate 71 spotted a strange confrontation about fifteen minutes ago. What you are seeing is live feed. There seems to be a man with a mask and a sword battling three individuals on top of a large sixteen-wheel truck. You heard me right, ladies and gentlemen. What you are witnessing is a battle on top of a moving vehicle going about forty-five miles per hour. Police have been dispatched to the scene. Is this The Masked Hero of New Orleans? Who are these other individuals? We're hoping to gain some answers over the next few minutes."

113

Jason heard the bell over the door chime. Melissa was in the parking lot, ripping off her server's apron and heading towards her motorcycle.

"Shit," Jason said, turning off the grill and throwing down his spatula.

"Heads up, Stacy," he said, passing her on his way around the counter, "I'm going to go help Nick."

"Huh?" she said. She had been ringing a customer out. Her eyes seemed to be glazed over. Had she really not heard the TV just now?

"Nick," he said, "Trouble. Mind the store."

She looked up at the TV, her mouth dropping open a little.

"No," she called after him.

"Stacy, you don't even have a weapon," he said, pushing the door open with his back.

"It's in the car," she said, taking off her apron as well.

"Wait…why is your crossbow in the car?" he asked, surprised and a bit alarmed.

Stacy shrugged, pushing past a customer on her way towards the door.

"Hey!" called a customer waiting on his pancakes, "Where the hell is everybody going? When am I going to get my food?"

"Cook it yourself," Jason said, flipping the sign outside the door to "Closed."

It was taking everything Nick had to keep from being pummeled, shot, or sliced to ribbons. These three were leagues ahead of any thugs or mercenaries he had fought before. These were trained killers - odd ones, but incredibly dangerous.

The big one was slow, but every time Nick landed a kick or a cut on him, he seemed completely un-fazed, and every once in a while, that shotgun would come forth and Nick would have to leap either upward or under the blast in order to avoid being splattered all over the highway. When Brick fired, the other two backed away in concert. The teamwork between the three of them was incredible.

The woman attacked with the ferocity of a wolverine, grunting and growling like a feral animal while keeping up a near constant barrage of punches and kicks. The spiked bands around her wrists and ankles had cut into Nick several times already as he dodged and weaved to avoid the full force of her blows. She seemed to only let up when one of the others was attacking.

The third one, the small thin man with the whip, moved with a silent grace that unnerved Nick greatly. His whip seemed to come alive in his hands, darting and swaying through the air and cutting swaths inches from Nick's vitals. Nick had received two blows from the barbed, razor-lined whip - one to his arm and another to his ribs. He suspected both cuts were bleeding heavily and would likely scar.

What scared Nick the most about the one Brick called Razorpriest was the way he seemed perfectly calm throughout the entire battle. He wasn't breathing heavily despite the movement, and his eyes never seemed to squint or narrow or betray any kind of struggle. He never spoke, nor made a sound of any kind, even when Nick had gotten close enough to kick him in the stomach earlier.

Who were these people? What were such obviously trained assassins doing ambushing him in the middle of broad daylight? He believed Raven had sent them, but he hoped to be able to get the answer from the horse's mouth before this encounter was over.

Assuming he survived long enough to do so.

Nick flipped backwards over Razorpriest's whip, dodging the weapon but still receiving a glancing kick from Bitch as he flew backwards. Nick landed within inches of the edge of the truck, already bracing himself, as Bitch was rushing forward with a scream on her lips.

He feigned a slash with his sword, counting on her ducking the anticipated strike. She did, and Nick met her chest with his knee. She grunted, the wind knocked out of her, and Nick took the opportunity to move past her and away from the precarious edge of the moving platform. Thank God the truck was no longer moving very fast.

Someone had staged this from the beginning. They knew he would be here, knew what route he would take on his way home. That meant they had been watching him for some time.

Great; exactly what he needed was another stalker.

At least these are human, he noted as he jumped over Razorpriest's whip and sliced its carrier in the face, leaving a small trail of blood across the man's cheek. Razorpriest staggered back for an instant but made no sound nor changed his facial expression from one of blank observation.

Nick carried his momentum forward towards Brick, kicking the shotgun to the side with one leg while planting his other on the big man's chest. He launched himself backwards, slashing Brick across the chest in a blow that he knew would be enough to leave most men bleeding and writhing on the ground.

Brick didn't budge. He grimaced and pointed his gun towards Nick soon after he landed.

Nick prepared to dodge the blow but stopped when Brick withdrew his weapon and holstered it instead.

That's when he heard the charge of a screaming banshee behind him.

Bitch hit him like a freight train, and Nick felt blood rush into his mouth as he smacked face-first into the surface below him. Short, quick punches began to rain into his kidneys as Bitch sat on top of him.

Nick yelled and tried to stand up, managing to rear up enough to quickly slide out from under her.

"Slippery little fuck," Bitch said, surprised at Nick's evasion.

He had to get out of here. He might not be outmatched on an even playing field, but Nick's combat style was dependent upon maneuverability, and he had precious little of it on the top of a truck.

The vehicle was in the far right lane. Nick thanked Heaven for small favors and made a dive for the shoulder, hoping the bushes would cushion his long, violent fall.

His body soared off of the vehicle but jerked backward before he could begin his descent. He felt himself slide back across the top of the truck.

The next thing he was aware of was excruciating pain. He looked down to see Razorpriest's whip wrapped around his ankle.

Razorpriest twitched his wrist, and somehow the vicious device came loose. Nick screamed in agony, clutching his shredded limb. His boot had taken much of the damage but not enough to shield his flesh from being sliced like cheddar through a cheese grater.

He looked up at them. Bitch was looming over him, breathing heavily and looking satisfied. Brick was smiling smugly. Razorpriest coiled the whip back into his hand and stood there, stone-faced.

This is not my month, Nick thought. I nearly get killed by a devil-worshiping wizard, I alienate the woman I love, and now I'm going to die at the hands of three comic-book villains on top of a speeding truck.

Nick heard sirens in the distance. The police were finally on their way, but he had a feeling they wouldn't be of any use against these three.

Then he heard something else - the roar of an engine quickly approaching. A motorcycle engine.

Thank God, Nick thought. The cavalry has arrived.

Melissa brought her bike to a stop on an overpass overlooking the highway. The truck was fast approaching below. She would only get one shot at this. She would either make it or end up in a broken heap on the pavement far below.

"Come on, come on, come on," she whispered to herself, climbing up on the edge of the concrete railing, gripping her staff tightly.

She locked her eyes on Nick - on him lying there with his sword pointed at three psychos ready to kill him. Melissa didn't know who they were and she didn't care. Her friend was in danger.

Before she could second-guess herself, she was airborne - the milliseconds between her jump from the railing and her feet hitting the top of the truck felt like an eternity, but fear turned to gratification when she felt the impact of her staff crashing into the collarbone of the woman looming over Nick.

Melissa brought her weapon and her attention behind her, daring the other two to attack.

"Moonbeam," said the big guy with the gun, "Byron said you might show up,"

"You fuck!" screamed the woman now lying on her back behind Melissa. "I'll fucking kill you!"

Melissa turned to her, her staff still focused on the others.

"You'll get your turn, Pebbles. Now shut your ugly mouth."

Nick carefully rose to his feet, placing as little pressure as possible on his injured left ankle.

"These guys are no joke, M. They're highly trained killers. Raven's, I assume."

Melissa turned her gaze back to Brick.

"Raven? That little shit sent you?"

Brick shrugged, "Doesn't matter who hired us. At the end of the day, we do what we want and we get what we want. The spoiled little rich kid wants us to keep an eye on you, but Byron is more interested in seeing what you've got. We ain't ever fought a damn superhero before. Couldn't resist the chance."

Melissa chuckled. "Well, Mr...."

"Brick, Bitch and Razorpriest," Nick informed her.

She turned to him quizzically.

"Seriously?"

Nick just shrugged.

Melissa shook her head and turned back to Brick.

"Well, Brick," she said, a hungry smile spreading across her lips. "You need to be a little more worried about me."

Stacy jumped out of the car as soon as Jason slowed down. She ran to the edge of the hill and immediately aimed her crossbow at the truck slowly passing below.

Three targets. Two men and a woman. The woman was getting up, but obviously hurt. Stacy had seen Melissa and Nick take on big men like the one with the gun before. There was something about the little one with the whip Stacy didn't trust. She took aim and fired.

The man actually turned in her direction a moment before the crossbow bolt hit him in the shoulder. He barely twitched when it did. She watched as the truck passed. The man's eyes stayed locked on her, and she could swear even from this distance that his ice-blue orbs were marking her for later. The feeling coursed through her like a shiver down her spine.

"Did you hit one of them? Get back in so we can make it down there!" Jason yelled.

Stacy turned, shaking off the strange sensation. That's when she felt a sharp metal tip suddenly dig into her neck.

Jason slammed the car door and approached carefully.

"Where the hell did you come from?" he asked.

Stacy turned her head slowly. A man of about 50 was holding the tip of a rapier to her throat. He was dressed in a mixture of Victorian and contemporary wear, with a shock of short white hair above a long scar covering half his face.

"Hello, Miss Cross, Mr. Dredd."

"Again," Jason said, "who the hell are you and how did you know we'd be here?"

"My name is Byron, Mr. Dreddowksi - and finding you was simple. You and your friends have become as predictable as the days of the week."

Jason stopped moving.

"You called me Dreddowski."

Byron stepped away from Stacy, swiping his sword downward with a flourish. Stacy immediately took a step back and leveled her crossbow at the stranger.

"Jason Dredd, formerly Jason Dreddowski, born in East Atlanta to a woman of African American and Polish descent and a father who left him in the cradle. Your brother Colin is on the run, currently in Missouri. Your mother is still missing, though easily retrievable to one with the proper resources, I assure you."

Byron then turned to Stacy.

"Stacy Elaine Cross, born to parents of Irish and Italian descent. Your father, while he lived, was an accomplished and awarded Air Force captain. He often took you and your sister on trips to the base, where he taught you marksmanship, basic self-defense, and how to pilot small aircraft."

"You're both officially listed as missing and presumed dead. You're working for wages under the table at The Roadside Diner. Well…you were until you ran out and left the store unattended just now."

Jason and Stacy shared a look.

"You've been following us?" Stacy asked.

"For Raven," Jason added, "right?"

Byron smiled.

"The circumstances of my employment are irrelevant. The fact is, for all your running and dodging from the rest of the world, I not only found you easily but was able to dig up more knowledge surrounding your short lives than likely even you know."

"Those are your men attacking our friends?" Jason asked.

"My associates, yes," Byron said with a proud nod.

"So what do you want?" Stacy asked.

"I want you to know you should be more careful covering your tracks if you want to stay below the world's radar, Miss Cross. And," Byron said, swiping his sword in the air and assuming a fencer's stance. "I want to know how long you can keep me from killing you."

Melissa whirled furiously in an attempt to force her three assailants to back off. She breathed a sigh of relief when Nick rolled around her and slashed at Brick. He did it from a sitting position, however. Nick was hurt badly and bleeding all over the place. They would have to end this soon and tend to his ankle if they didn't want him to bleed to death. Poor Nick was getting the worst of all of their fights lately.

She couldn't help but feel exhilarated as she dodged, parried, and struck at these three incredible adversaries. She hadn't felt this challenged in a long time, and it was a wonderful feeling despite the danger - or perhaps because of it.

The wind whipped through her hair, and she yelled exuberantly as she thrust the butt of her staff towards Razorpriest. The odd man backed up a step. He would have retaliated, but Nick jumped up and hobbled a step towards him, jabbing his sword in the way of Razorpriest's whip, preventing a strike against Melissa.

"Look at me, cunt. I'm gonna cut your face off," Bitch called towards her.

Melissa turned her attention fully towards the woman.

"Damn. Someone's got a dirtier mouth than I do."

Bitch let out a yell and a leaping kick towards Melissa. Melissa dodged it and punched Bitch in the stomach, but the woman was still on the offensive the moment she hit the ground. She let loose a right hook and then a left, taking advantage of the close quarters and not allowing Melissa a chance to use her staff.

Melissa blocked with her left hand, but Bitch's left hook hit her square in her collarbone.

"Tit for tat," Bitch said, bringing a roundhouse kick towards Melissa's left side.

Melissa surprised Bitch by taking the blow and grabbing her leg. Bitch struggled, but Melissa held the leg strong.

"See? You said 'tit.' Didn't your momma teach you to talk like a lady?"

She kneed Bitch in the groin, making her stumble back a step. Melissa then let go of her leg and whacked Bitch in the side of the head with her staff.

To Melissa's dismay, Bitch simply winced and rolled with the momentum of the blow, bringing her upper body down and to the right, tucking in and then charging at Melissa.

Melissa's eyes widened. The crazy bitch was going to knock them both off the truck.

Moving purely on instinct, Melissa jumped upward, spreading her legs outward and vaulting over Bitch.

Bitch howled and flailed her arms. Melissa spun around and caught her by the shirt, holding her as she leaned out over the ground far below.

"Learn some manners and get a better makeup artist, Pebbles. Less is definitely more," Melissa said and then shoved the woman hard.

She didn't even bother to see where and how Bitch landed. She turned towards Nick, who was surprisingly holding his own against the other two even with a hobbled foot.

"Who else wants some fashion advice?"

Byron was untouchable. Jason couldn't even begin to swing his chain before the man sliced or jabbed his exposed arms, eliciting a cry of pain every time. He would dance in close enough to strike and then double-step back in an instant. Jason had watched fencing on TV several times, but this was something else. Byron was a fencer on speed.

Stacy's shots were being batted away like flies. He even knocked one away that was aimed at the back of his neck. The man hadn't even broken a sweat.

"Really, you two. I know you're not the naturals your friends are, but you really must learn to be more adaptable in your styles."

Jason, fed up with Byron's games, took another piercing blow but this time stepped into it, gritting his teeth as the blade bit in deep.

Byron widened his eyes, smiling in approval.

Ignoring the man's smugness, Jason swung his right arm forward, attempting to wrap his chain around the man's head.

But Byron withdrew his blade and pirouetted under Jason's arm in one fluid motion, immediately stepping back out of Jason's range.

"Nice, Mr. Dredd, but some obstacles cannot be overcome with brute force. Learn to be crafty and unpredictable, or one day you'll be lying in a pool of your own blood."

Byron's sword arm suddenly shot up, seeming to move almost independent of the rest of his body. The blade deflected another of Stacy's crossbow bolts.

"And you, Miss Cross," Byron said, quickly moving towards her with his blade in the lead, "need to learn to be less reliant on a single ranged weapon."

Stacy inhaled sharply and backed up as Bryon moved at her. He came in high, but at the last instant slashed low, cutting Stacy across both of her knees.

She struggled to pull another bolt from her side pouch, but Byron met her hand in a flash, removing the bolt from her fingers and flinging it away before it could reach her weapon.

"See? A crossbow is powerful but far too slow to reload. You need a backup weapon. Might I suggest a rapier?"

Jason took advantage of Byron's distraction, swinging five feet of his chain at Byron's leg.

Again without looking at the projectile hurling towards him, Byron threw his sword to the ground.

Jason's chain fell limp. He looked at the dirt in shock. Byron had thrown his sword directly at the middle of a single link of chain, stopping it in its tracks.

"How the hell…" Jason muttered.

Byron backed away from his weapon and his opponents, reaching into his belt and pulling forth a small pistol.

"Sadly disappointing, my friends. You've got a long way to go if you want to be a match for someone like me."

He pointed the gun towards the sky and pulled the trigger. A single flare rocketed into the air, lighting a bright trail above them.

Byron stepped back slowly.

"Until next time Mr. Dredd, Miss Cross. And there will be a next time. Remember my advice, and try not to be killed by common street thugs before we meet again."

He turned and ran into the underbrush and down the hill.

Jason and Stacy simply watched him go. Finally Jason turned to her, his arms sore from all the pokes and cuts he had received.

"What the hell was that?" he said incredulously.

Stacy shook her head. She pulled her eyes away from Byron, locking them on the rapier he had left behind, still stuck in the dirt. She took a step forward and pulled it from the ground.

It was a magnificent weapon, light as a feather, yet obviously strong enough to stop the momentum from Jason's chain.

"Stacy?" Jason called to her.

She studied the blade a moment longer before looking up at him.

"Let's go," he said, wrapping his weapon around his arm.

She nodded, and followed him with rapier in tow.

Nick and Melissa had Brick and Razopriest on the defensive when Razorpriest suddenly looked towards the sky and put a hand on Brick's heavy shoulder.

"Huh?" the big man said, looking at his partner then at the sky.

"Crap," Brick said, holstering his shotgun. He hopped back onto the cab of the truck, kneeling down and hammering twice on the roof with his fist.

Razorpriest stood in front of Nick and Melissa, whip menacingly ready.

The truck then began to slow down.

"Well, it's been fun kicking your ass for a while," Brick sighed, cracking his knuckles.

"Like hell," Melissa said. "I kicked your girlfriend off the truck, and you would have been crying like a baby in a few minutes."

Brick chuckled. "You wish."

"Even Silent Bob there would be crying for his momma," she added.

Razorpriest didn't seem to notice the comment, but he did straighten up and latch the whip to his belt.

Brick laughed harder.

"You're a hoot, Melissa. Not to mention a fine piece of ass. Too bad we have to go. Once your hero friend was out of the way, you and I could have had a little wrestling match of our own."

"Dream on, douche bag," Melissa said with an air of disgust.

Razorpriest hopped off the truck. He seemed in a hurry to respond to the flare.

Brick shrugged. "Your loss, sweetheart. Don't get too comfortable, kids. We'll be seeing you again real soon."

He too jumped off the truck as the vehicle came to a stop.

"Silent Bob. That was a good one, Priesty," they heard Brick chuckle to his partner as they walked away.

Melissa shook her head and then turned back towards Nick. He was sitting down. She could tell he was grimacing in pain underneath his mask.

As she knelt down to help him, they both heard the door of the truck open and shut. A small chubby man ran out, waving his arms back and forth at the police cars coming to a stop behind the truck.

"They made me do it!" he shouted. "They made me do it!"

"The po-po ought to catch those assholes," Melissa said. They hadn't even noticed the police following them - nor the helicopters circling overhead. They had been a little too distracted.

"Not if they're Raven's. We should be a bit more concerned about them catching us," Nick said to her.

Heavy footsteps surrounded the truck below them. They could hear radios blaring police codes.

They were surrounded.

"This is Detective Cross! Kick your weapons over the side and then move to the edge of the vehicle with your hands up!" issued a loud voice from below.

"Stacy's cousin. Crap," Melissa said.

But then another sound erupted out over the blare of the sirens and helicopters. A loud hiss and a flash of light emanated from a nearby hilltop. An instant later, two police cars exploded behind them.

"Holy hell!" Melissa shouted.

Nick shielded his face from the heat of the blast.

"Someone covering for the bounty hunters. That was a rocket blast! We have to help them!" he screamed.

Melissa stood up and surveyed the situation. Most of the cops surrounding the truck had scrambled back or towards their comrades who had been closer to the vehicles. She could see a few lying on the concrete, dead or at least injured.

"Like hell, Nick. We've got to get out of here," she said, picking him up and tossing his slender body over her shoulder.

"Melissa! Stop! I have to help them!"

"Shut up, Nick! You're more likely to get shot!"

She jumped down to the cab, then to the hood, then to the ground, grunting due to the added weight. She could see a familiar red station wagon approaching from the west-bound lane. Jason and Stacy had arrived.

She ran towards them, jumping over the median. She ducked as she heard another rocket blast behind her. The helicopter exploded above them.

Jason hopped out of the car, and Melissa could see the reflection of the flaming wreckage in his shades. The chopper smashed into the hillside near the source of the rocket blast.

She tossed Nick into the back of the car and then jumped in beside him.

"Book it while we have the chance!" she yelled.

Seconds later they were racing down the highway, away from the carnage. The only present means of tailing them, the helicopter, had been destroyed.

"What the hell was that?" Jason said, pounding the steering wheel.

"Professionals," Nick said, holding Stacy's jacket around his leg.

"Raven's," Melissa added.

"I figured that much. We were attacked, too. Some guy named Byron. He looked like a reject from the Count of Monte Cristo," Jason said.

"That must have been the one with the rocket launcher," Nick said, "Unless there was a fifth one."

"Well, let's hope the cops grab them. What's left of the cops," Melissa said, running a hand through her hair and letting her nerves settle. She chose not to mention Thomas Cross's presence at the scene in case he had been one of the casualties.

"Otherwise, we've got yet another reason to watch our backs."

14

Detective Cross sat with his back to one of the few cruisers left intact from the blast. An EMT was examining his leg, which had apparently caught a small bit of shrapnel. Not enough to impair movement but certainly enough to hurt like hell.

"So we know that was that Hero kid up there, but any idea who those other psychos were?" the EMT asked him.

Tom shook his head.

"No. No clue."

Truth was, that was a lie. He knew one of those "psychos" alright. Melissa Lunar Moonbeam. It wouldn't have taken much to confirm his suspicions that Stacy's friends were involved in the Masked Hero case, but this sure as hell pushed those suspicions over the edge into incontrovertible fact. Nick or Nick Moonbeam, or Just-Plain-Nick, or whatever the hell his name was - was The Masked Hero - or what Tom preferred to call, "The Masked Suspect."

As the EMT worked, Tom remained silent and surveyed the scene. The RPGs had come from the hillside overlooking the highway. Whoever had fired them was long gone. Yet there had to be something left....

There. Tom caught a glint of metal in the tall grass. He brought his comm-device to his mouth and nearly called out to his unit when he noticed something odd. The glint of metal was moving.

The object seemed to almost stand up a bit, yet remained hunched as if attempting to remain hidden. It must have been somewhat successful, as it appeared to move only as Thomas noticed the figure, probably because he had been looking right at it.

It shambled quickly up the hill and away from the highway, afternoon sun continuing to glint off of what looked like metal armor.

Tom was reminded of footage of Bigfoot he had seen. That improbable thing moving just beyond the range of common perception, yet there if one had the eyes to see.

He remembered the taloned footprints found at the scene of some of the homeless murders. The long, curved scratch marks on the walls and floor, sometimes even on the ceiling.

There was something following Nick and the rest of them. Something Thomas couldn't quite convince himself was human.

The four of them huddled around the television, watching the footage repeat over and over again. Nick battling the three bounty hunters. Melissa leaping onto the truck. The rocket blasts that claimed the lives of five police officers, one television journalist, a cameraman and a pilot.

They watched as Stacy's cousin, Detective Cross, held a brief press conference recounting what little detail the police knew about those involved in the events, which wasn't much.

Eight dead. Eight innocent people whose lives were taken in what seemed to be a game to those people.

"Bounty hunters. You're sure that's what they were?" Stacy asked.

"Yeah," Jason said, "People like that…trained killers like that…only someone like Raven would know where to find those kinds of people."

"They were obviously not from around here," Nick added.

"You mean planet Earth?" Melissa joked.

"The woman seemed to have a Chinese or Korean accent, you said," Jason continued, "and the man that attacked us, the one I think is the leader, had a German or Austrian accent."

"The big one sounded American. Canadian, maybe. And the other one…" Nick said.

"My god, that one creeped me out. The way he looked at me after I shot at him…" Stacy said, wrapping her arms around herself.

"Yeah, there was something about that guy that wasn't right," Melissa agreed.

"And that weapon…" Nick said, clutching his ankle. Jason had taken a look at it earlier, and the damage was not as bad as Nick had thought. It would probably scar, but nothing vital had been severed.

In fact, Jason commented on how impossible it seemed that Nick had only suffered surface wounds if the weight of his entire body had really been jerked back by a whip lined with razor blades.

"Whoever they are, I don't think they're content to go by Raven's orders alone," Melissa said. "They basically told us as much. Raven may have hired someone capable to keep tabs on us, but these creeps apparently couldn't keep their curiosity to themselves. Who can blame them? We are kind of awesome."

Nick chuckled then immediately drew in a sharp breath as a new wave of pain hit him.

"But if they've been watching us for very long, what else have they seen?" he said through gritted teeth.

They all let that sink in for a moment.

"David. The Whisper. Maybe even our trip to Alabama." Melissa said softly. "Holy shit, Nick, I didn't even think about that."

"Byron knew where my brother was. So he had to have been tracking us at least since Colin...got hurt," Jason said.

"Guys," Melissa said gravely. "I hate to say this, but between these new guys, Raven, The Whisper, and now probably the authorities after us...this may have be the perfect time for us to lose our jobs."

"You're suggesting we lay low," Jason said.

"Couldn't be a bad idea," Melissa agreed.

"The rest of you should stay here as much as possible, I agree. I'll have to keep my head down even more now," Nick said.

"Why, Nick? Why us and not you?" Stacy said, sounding displeased.

"Because I can't just...stop, Stacy. I don't wear this mask because it keeps my face warm. I do it because I have to help people."

"You don't have to do a damn thing," Stacy argued.

"Say it, sister," Melissa chimed in.

"Yes, I do," Nick countered. "I can't just hide when danger comes. I'm trying my hardest to be what people want me to be, and that means I have to be there for them no matter what."

"But you could get hurt, Nick," Stacy said, obviously agitated. "You did get hurt. What happens when you get shot next time? Or that whip wraps around your neck? Or The Whisper cuts your arm off? You're good, Nick, but you're not that good. In fact, you seem to be getting your ass handed to you an awful lot lately."

"Ooh, snap!" Melissa grinned.

"No," Jason said sternly. "Nick is probably right."

Melissa looked at him in surprise, and Stacy shot him an angry look. Nick himself just sat back in his chair, looking uncomfortable.

"Nick has a job to do. He took up a hard mantle when he decided to become The Hero instead of running from the label. I told him he was doing the right thing then, and I'll say it again now. It would be selfish of us to tell him to stay," Jason said.

"Then maybe it's past damn time to be selfish!" Stacy yelled, jumping to her feet. She glared at Nick and then spun around. Blitz cowered and quickly ran out of her way with his tail between his legs. She stomped up the steps and slammed her door with enough force to make the house shake.

"What…the…hell," Melissa whispered, looking at Nick and Jason with her mouth open.

"Seriously," Jason said, "what happened to her? It's like she's angry all the time now. Melissa, do you still hear her toss and turn at night?"

"And yell, and cry, and shake the bed frame," Melissa answered.

They looked to Nick for an answer. He knew her better than anyone, but he only sat there, his shoulders slumped. He looked almost as grumpy as Stacy did.

Nick had given up trying to help her. He was convinced now that anything he said or did could only make things worse between them.

So, instead, he changed the subject.

"Halloween is in two days. I have a feeling this year will be particularly bad."

Jason sighed, knowing that Nick would have nothing else to say on the subject of Stacy.

"Probably. All the vandals come out to play."

"Aw, shit. I should have saved the thing about us hiding till after Halloween," Melissa pouted.

"You'll have to be content passing out candy," Nick said.

"Grrr. I hate kids," she said.

"Too bad. It won't kill you to play domestic for a night," Jason said.

The next morning, Melissa handed the phone to Nick while he was sitting on the back porch, looking out at the lake and contemplating the unnerving speed at which his ankle was healing.

"Patty Cake," Melissa said. It was her nickname for Patricia. That and Punky Brewster.

"Hey," Nick said, taking the phone from Melissa.

"Nick," Patricia said on the other end, "Hey."

Nick sat back in his chair.

"You okay?"

He heard her pause and take a deep breath.

"I've...I've been seeing things, Nick," she said.

Now Nick was concerned. Usually Patricia was as calm as a cucumber. Now he could hear the unease in her voice as plain as day. She sounded even more scared than the day they confronted Sam.

"What kind of things?"

"Benjamin," she answered.

Nick stopped breathing for a moment.

"What do you mean? Is he okay?" he asked, suddenly afraid for Patricia's little brother.

"Yeah, he's fine. That's the weird thing. His condition hasn't improved at all, but...I see him, up and walking around. At night sometimes. Or right before dusk. I'll just turn around and there he is, or open my eyes and he'll be standing beside me."

Nick didn't know what to say, but he did remember the sensation of having his hand brushed while at Benjamin's bedside.

"His mouth moves," Patricia continued, "like he's trying to say something. The first few times I saw him, I didn't hear anything at all, but lately I've been hearing sounds. Not words...yet. Just sounds."

"So what do you think it is? Do you really think it's him?" Nick asked, his mind whirling. He had seen too much in his short life to doubt something like this.

"I don't know, Nick!" Patricia said, her voice catching in her throat, nearly sounding like a sob.

"I just...needed to talk to somebody," she said.

"I'm here. You know you can tell me anything. Do you need me to come down there?" he asked.

"No, no. That's too far to come just because I'm going crazy. I'm alright, really. It hasn't tried to hurt me, it just…. Nick, I can't shake the feeling that it's trying to tell me something important," she said.

Nick looked out at the lake, continuing to listen. He didn't fail to notice that Patricia called her vision "it" instead of "him." For her to be so terrified of something that looked like her beloved brother….

"And for some reason I feel like it has something to do with you."

"What?" he asked in surprise.

"Yeah. When he's there I get this…feeling. Like I used to get when I would have those dreams I told you about. Haven't had those in a while, by the way. But I'd get this sense like you were in the room. I could almost feel you standing there. I think it did that - like it's trying to tell me something important about you."

15

Patricia hadn't been able to say more than that. Her feeling had been just that - a feeling. Like an odd itching in the back of her skull, she had said. Nick didn't understand why anything threatening would come at him through Patricia of all people. He was constantly worried about The Whisper hurting Stacy or one of the others, but Patricia was three states away and only occasionally kept in contact with him. What would make her different?

The thought actually comforted Nick. Whatever Patricia was experiencing, it likely had nothing to do with him, and that was definitely a good thing for both of them. Being around him was a dangerous position to be in, and Nick had that notion verified while they were watching the news the evening after Patricia's call.

"Police are still on the lookout for these five individuals, including the so called, 'Masked Hero,' witnessed at the scene of yesterday's mysterious freeway skirmish which left eight people dead and more hospitalized. Police claim that this sketch of a tall blonde woman matches witness descriptions of the nightclub incident months ago that left three people dead and an enormous mystery plaguing New Orleans City Police."

Nick looked over at Melissa. Her eyes were wide and her hand froze in front of her face, a fork carrying a wad of ramen noodles hovering before her lips.

"In that incident, witnesses described a large man wearing what appeared to be metal armor attacking and murdering the club's patrons, while two unidentified individuals - a tall blonde woman and a large African American male - fought the armored assailant and later escaped. Could the two incidents be related? Both involve unknown assailants of strange appearance, and both have police baffled."

Now Nick glared at Jason.

"You fought The Whisper and didn't tell me?" he said angrily.

"Yeah," Jason said, sighing, "we didn't want you to worry."

"And you beat him?" Nick asked incredulously.

"Well, we didn't so much beat him as…run away from him and make him crash into a truck," Melissa said, eying Nick sheepishly.

Nick didn't know what to say. His fears were confirmed. The Whisper wasn't going to be content with simply going after him. It was stalking his friends as well.

The next night was Halloween. Stacy was standing in the foyer silently carving a pumpkin. She hadn't said a word to any of them all night. Nick noticed Blitz going out of his way to avoid her. He didn't like the look of that one bit.

Jason was cooking dinner. Lasagna and roast chicken. The leftovers would be waiting for Nick in the fridge when he got home. He couldn't help but feel a bit guilty for leaving his friends on a holiday, but he had a duty to perform, and besides, the mood in the house was less than festive, what with Stacy more sullen than ever and the four of them on the lamb.

The fact of which had led them to agree that Melissa, who had been left with door-duty, had to dress up.

Nick was not amused when he finally saw her idea for a costume.

She was dressed in black and wearing a small black mask over her mouth and nose. A cheap plastic sword was strapped to her back.

"My name's Nick. I don't remember anything. I've got a dog and a sword and an emo haircut. I fight like a freak from a French Canadian circus, and I sit around and sulk a lot. Wah wah wah. I'm so cool and mysterious and afraid of girls. Wah wah wah," Melissa said, standing in front of him, waving her hands back and forth dramatically.

"That's just effing hilarious," Nick said, his voice dripping with sarcasm.

"Hey, I'm not going to let you be the only one having fun tonight, you freaking tool," Melissa shot back, punching him in the arm.

Nick was already dressed and armed and ready to head out the door. He walked over to Stacy and put a hand on her shoulder. She shrugged it off immediately.

"I'm sorry, Stace. I really wish I could stay here with you tonight, but…."

"Run away, Nick. I don't expect anything more from you anymore," she said, not taking her eyes away from the pumpkin.

Nick looked at the floor, wishing he knew the right thing to say.

The doorbell rang. Their first trick-or-treaters had arrived.

"Hot damn! Time to scare some toddlers!" Melissa said merrily, skipping past Nick and Stacy with a basket of candy in her hand.

She opened the door to a scene of a werewolf, a witch, and a Power Ranger. They all looked up at her and smiled.

"Trick or Treat!"

"Wow, you're supposed to be The Masked Hero!" the little boy in the werewolf costume said.

"Yeah, but don't let the news fool you kids. He's a jerk. Lots of people can beat him up," Melissa said, handing out candy.

Blitz trotted out the door in front of Nick.

"Ooh, doggy!" the little girl said, "can I pet him?"

"Sure, he's a sweety," Nick said, moving out onto the porch beside Melissa.

The kids looked up at him, confused.

"So you're supposed to be The Hero, too?" The Power Ranger said.

"Supposed to be," Nick said, "so do you think I did a good job?"

"Yeah," the werewolf said. "I think you make a good Hero."

"Gag me with a spoon," Melissa leaned over and whispered to him.

"You're too skinny, though," the little girl said, her arm wrapped around Blitz.

"Hah!" Melissa burst out laughing.

"Thanks," Nick said, shaking his head and walking down the steps.

"Don't get eaten up by any ghouls or ghosts or demons. Wink wink," Melissa called after him, actually saying "wink wink."

Nick waved and walked off down the driveway, Blitz in tow.

Demons. After last night's revelation and Stacy's cruel words, he actually hoped he did run into one.

He had some frustration to burn.

Stacy watched Nick go. It seemed she was doomed to always see him walk away from her. No matter how much she loved him, no matter how much she showed him he didn't have to be alone, Nick would never care. He only cared about protecting himself. He only cared about being a hero, even though he had proven to her he was a failure as a man.

She was done with him. She was done with holding on to the futile dream of having a knight in shining armor. Nick would never be that. The few ex-boyfriends that she had long since left behind certainly weren't. No one she had ever met could meet that standard. In fact, she now believed that true love couldn't exist. It was all a selfish lie. Just two people fooling themselves for the sake of security, or sex, or image.

That life she had dreamed of, of living a constant adventure and having friends who truly needed her, had turned out to be a lie as well. She thought once that she had found it alongside Nick and Melissa and Jason, but every time things came down to the wire, every time they were threatened or challenged in some way, it was always the three of them who ran ahead to face their enemies and Stacy who lagged hopelessly behind.

They didn't need her. Nick was powerful but emotionally crippled. Melissa was arrogant and stupid. Jason was selfish and single-minded. None of them looked at her the way they looked at each other. All she represented to them was a burden.

She looked down at the pumpkin, watching her hands carve the final cuts into its surface. She removed the chunk she had just carved out of one of the eyes and then placed a small candle inside, lighting it with a match.

After replacing the lid of the pumpkin, Stacy watched the match continue to burn. She watched as the flame neared her fingertips and then began to burn them. Her skin turned black, and as it did, her thoughts did as well.

She threw the match to the floor. It smoldered and then went out, leaving a small black stain on the linoleum.

She felt something dark take over inside herself. Her body switched to auto-pilot, and her head turned to the end table beside the couch to her left. A paper weight, a large smooth stone Jason had found beside the lake, was lying there on top of a newspaper. Her hand clasped around it. She did not take the time to ask herself why. She was beyond caring at this point.

"Hey Stace, come look at these kids a few houses over. Are those the Spice Girls? What are we, in the '90s?" Melissa called to her.

Melissa was propped up against the front window with her back to her. Stacy froze for a moment. Her heart beat faster.

Melissa. Stronger than her. Prettier than her. Better in every way.

Her palms were sweating. Her knuckles clenched the rock until they were white.

The back of Melissa's arrogant head called to her.

Nick was probably really in love with her.

Stacy felt her feet move beneath her.

"Stacy, leave the stupid pumpkin alone for…" Melissa said impatiently, beginning to turn.

Two seconds later, blood was splattered on the window.

"I have to get my head in the game," Nick said to Blitz. The two of them were casually walking through a subdivision. They had been making their way from neighborhood to neighborhood for several hours, looking for trouble and not finding any. All there was to see were kids cavorting from house to house, protective parents watching them from idling cars, and the occasional teenager out for a spin.

"Stacy isn't my concern. She can't be anymore. The more I inject myself into her life the worse it's going to be for her. So whatever she's going through right now…she'll have to go through by herself. Or the others can help. They don't have demons and bounty hunters and psychotic magicians stalking them."

Nick knew that wasn't true, but he found it easier to single himself out. Everything was a bit easier to handle when it was all about him. If he convinced himself that he was the only one in harm's way, the fear wouldn't overwhelm him. Otherwise…he didn't think he could handle a life where he might lose the only people he cared about at any given moment. He just wasn't strong enough for that.

"I need to be out here. Every night. Alone…except for you, of course," he said. Blitz looked up at him and gave him a slight wag of the tail.

But Nick knew he was fooling himself there as well. The world didn't need The Hero. It had been getting by before he had arrived and it would get by after he was gone. No, he knew that the truth was that he needed it. Putting on that mask had become his own personal method of running away - of focusing on the moment instead of the insurmountable perils of his incomplete life.

He wanted to help people. That was in his blood. But every person he saved, defended, or aided would die someday anyway. In this increasingly violent world, many of them would likely die in some horrible way no matter what he did. He wasn't really anything special. He was, after all, only a guy with a sword.

"And a dog," Nick said, reaching down to scratch Blitz behind the ears.

Blitz's presence reminded him that things weren't bad, no matter how he tried to make them that way. For every enemy he had a beloved friend, someone who would likely die for him just as he would for them.

So why didn't he just stay with them? If his role as The Hero was really as limited as he thought, why didn't he just abandon the mask once and for all and be satisfied with living a normal life? As normal a life as people like them could lead, anyway.

Because he was addicted. Some people drank too much. Others watched too much TV. Nick went out at night and swung a sword at people.

He loved it. He loved to fight. He loved to run. He loved to just sit in the shadows and watch people. It made him feel indestructible, but more importantly it made him forget all the missing pieces of himself and all the horrors that lurked just a step behind him.

Or in front of him. The Pull had not gone away. It was so faint now he could barely feel it, but it was there. It was still pulling him east. Back to Atlanta and whatever he had once failed to find there.

Nick stepped aside as a truck passed by. In its bed were a vampire, a scarecrow and a tiger - of the fifth grade variety. They were smiling and digging in their candy bags without a care in the world.

Nick suddenly felt stupid for letting the joy of the night get away from him.

"Melissa's right. I am a whiney bitch," he said shaking his head and stretching his arms above him.

"What say we go back home and see if we can't have a little fun before the others go to bed?" Nick asked Blitz.

Blitz panted happily. Nick turned to cut through the woods but paused as he heard the sound of laughter and breaking glass from the house behind him.

It was an open house for sale. A big two story with a huge bay window. It was the window that had shattered. He could see several figures running about inside.

Teenagers, Nick realized - kids whose idea of Halloween fun was to find as many things to break as they could.

He sighed.

"Looks like this night isn't going to be uneventful after all."

He and Blitz quietly made their way across the street and up the driveway. The kids were on the second floor, and Nick had no trouble soundlessly making his way into the house and up the stairs.

There were four of them, and all of them were together in a room adjacent to the master bedroom. Nick sent Blitz to the door that led to the room from the hallway, while he crept through the bedroom.

The kids - four boys - were merrily smashing everything they could find. A full length mirror cracked in dozens of places as one boy hit it with an empty paint bucket. Another kid was kicking a toilet, trying to dislodge it from the wall.

They all froze when Blitz suddenly let out an angry bark. They turned to see the dog standing there in the darkened doorway. His back was arched and his teeth were bared threateningly.

"How do kids go so easily from collecting candy to smashing private property?" Nick said from the opposite doorway.

The kids gasped and turned to him.

"Shit!" one of the kids said in a high-pitched shriek.

Nick drew his sword and held it in the dim light of the streetlight outside.

"You know that for every broken window I find, I'm going to have to cut off one of your toes."

The boys all bunched together in the center of the room, alternating frightened glances between the angry dog and the man with the sword.

"P...please. We didn't mean to do anything ba...bad," one of the boys sputtered.

"You mean you just accidentally threw a paint can at this mirror?" Nick replied, motioning towards the pile of broken glass on the floor.

"No, I mean we...we weren't trying to hurt anyone. It's Halloween...nobody lives here. We just...wanted to have some fun."

Nick stared at the boys long and hard. Two of them jumped as Blitz barked and took a step towards them.

Finally, Nick shrugged and sheathed his weapon.

"Fair enough," he said.

The boys seemed stunned.

"We…we can go?" one of them asked.

"Yeah," Nick said, "I'm trespassing too, aren't I?"

The boys relaxed a bit. One of them even laughed nervously.

But then Nick darted forward in a flash, grabbing one of the boys by the collar and yanking him about an inch and a half from Nick's masked face.

"But if I ever catch any of you breaking things that aren't yours again," he said as menacingly as he could manage. "I'll have my dog there chew your legs off."

The boy he was holding whimpered.

"Blitz, let them through," Nick said. The dog immediately dropped his threatening posture and trotted into the room.

The other three boys scampered out quickly. Nick released the boy in his grip.

"Sorry, Mr. Hero," the boy said before chasing after his friends.

Nick had a feeling that this was one Hero encounter he would not be hearing about on the evening news.

He chuckled to himself as he listened to the four of them stomp out of the house and then run down the street as fast as they could.

"Okay, you have to admit that was funny," Nick said to Blitz.

Blitz gave a small whine and headed out of the room.

"Hey, it's not like I would have really hurt them," Nick said defensively.

He looked around the room he was in. It seemed to be an enormous bathroom. There was a garden tub on one wall and a toilet in a small nook in the corner, but otherwise the space looked more like a big walk-in closet. Cabinets were suspended from the ceiling on every wall but the one above the tub. The six-foot mirror in front of him was in ruin, but Nick could still see himself in the reflection of the glass shards left in the frame.

"Some hero you are," he said to his reflection. "You nearly made that kid pee himself."

He felt something as he looked at himself - a small tug from within. It was The Pull. It had just shifted, like a child kicking in its mother's womb.

"What the…" Nick exclaimed.

An image flashed into his head. Nick took a step back from the mirror. The image appeared again, but this time Nick held onto it.

He closed his eyes and focused.

There was a tall dark figure standing in a doorway. It looked like the entrance to a house. The figure itself was shrouded in darkness somehow, even though Nick could make out the doorway very distinctly. Somehow, that doorway looked familiar. He tried to take a step back in his mind to see if he could get a more complete view of the scene. It worked, and to his right Nick spotted a red shutter. It was blood red, just like the eyes of the figure standing there, he now could see. Red pinpricks of light, like burning embers floating in darkness. He knew that face. He knew who those eyes belonged to. If only he could remember.

Nick was shaken from his trance by the sound of Blitz howling in panic. He opened his eyes…

…only to see eyes of purple fire and a flaming grin staring from behind him in the broken mirror.

Nick spun around but not quickly enough to stop The Whisper from slamming him into the mirror, shattering the rest of it and leaving a large dent in the wall behind it.

"No!" Nick yelled, feeling himself hurled through the air as The Whisper tossed him across the room.

"Not now!" Nick screamed, planting his feet on the wall and running across to the cabinets on the opposite corner.

He didn't have time for this. He had almost remembered the source of The Pull. Nick shoved off of the wall, slashing furiously at his metal nemesis. The Whisper blocked with two bladed fingers and turned to face Nick as the boy flew over him, landing on the other side of the room.

"It was you who took my memory, wasn't it?" Nick asked the monster, bringing his sword in front of him.

"You did this to me!!" he screamed, rushing forward to attack.

The Whisper let out a raspy laugh, blocking Nick's charge and not budging an inch.

"*Been watching*," it said to him. The monster slashed outward with both hands and moved towards Nick, mowing forward with first one fist and then the other.

"Should have kept a closer eye on her," it said as Nick jumped back towards the wall.

Nick froze. The Whisper only glared at him and watched as realization dawned on his face.

"Stacy," Nick said, suddenly making sense of her strange change in behavior, "you were inside her, weren't you? The same way you were with me. You made her this way," Nick said, edging towards the doorframe. Suddenly his rage was gone. All he wanted was to get home. To run to her.

The Whisper merely smiled, and then opened his mouth wide and charged forward. Nick could not move fast enough to dodge the charging demon. The Whisper hit him head-on and slammed him into and through the sheetrock wall.

Nick grunted and clenched his teeth as he felt himself carried over the railing of the balcony overlooking the downstairs. The two of them flew through the air. Dear lord, this was going to hurt, Nick thought.

He was right.

The Whisper slammed him down onto the kitchen island counter below.

"*Too slow*," it said, its face directly in front of Nick's.

The Whisper then slid Nick across the counter, hurling him like a projectile into the open pantry nearby. Nick slammed into some shelves set into the wall and then landed on the ground in a heap amid a pile of broken shelving and sheetrock.

He could barely move. The wind was knocked out of him. He wasn't even capable of lifting his sword. The demon could finish him off easily if it wanted to.

The Whisper walked over to him casually, almost nonchalantly. It leaned over him, putting its hands on its knees.

"*Too weak*," it said to him in its strange mind-speak.

"Why," Nick coughed, "why won't you just kill me?"

The Whisper laughed and pointed a bladed finger at Nick's chest. He pressed the finger into Nick's flesh, making him scream in pain.

"*Mine*," it responded.

And then it stood back up and simply walked away, not running or darting into the shadows like it usually did. It was a statement, Nick knew, that no matter what he did, the demon would always be stronger.

After a few moments, Blitz trotted into the pantry, none the worse for wear.

Nick grimaced and sat up. Nothing important seemed broken. He didn't know how that was possible, but he could move now with little difficulty. He just felt a little more bruised and cut up than he had twenty minutes ago.

"Thanks for the help," Nick said to Blitz, placing his hand on the dog's shoulder and using him as a support to get back to his feet.

Nick looked at the dog. Blitz seemed genuinely remorseful, his brown eyes cast up at Nick as if asking for forgiveness.

"Nah, I'm glad you ran. I don't want you in between me and that thing."

Nick limped out of the pantry. His back felt as if it had been hit by a wrecking ball. He looked at the cracked kitchen counter and up towards the broken railing. He supposed a wrecking ball wasn't too far off.

"No time to be hurt," he said. "Gotta get back to Stacy."

Nick forced himself into a run. His heart told him that whatever it was he feared, he might already be too late.

16

Melissa woke up to an intense pain in her wrists. Thin rope dug into her skin, nearly cutting off her circulation. Her ankles felt bound together as well. She was sitting against a wall next to someone. She opened her eyes. Jason was next to her, his eyes locked on the person standing at the other end of the room.

Melissa turned a cold glare towards Stacy.

"What the hell did you do?"

Stacy was standing there with her crossbow trained on the two of them. Her eyes were crazed and her clothes and hair were a mess. She looked as if she had just rolled down a flight of stairs.

"She knocked us both out," Jason said, "hit you with that rock I found, and then clubbed me in the forehead with it when I came to investigate. And then she somehow dragged us both up to the attic and tied us up."

Melissa looked around. They did indeed seem to be in the attic. She didn't think she had ever actually been up here. What a strange reason to make her first visit.

"You carried us up here? How the hell…."

"Don't you fucking doubt me," Stacy shot back.

"Stacy. Nobody doubts you. Now calm down and tell us what's wrong," Jason said.

"She's crazy, that's what's wrong," Melissa said.

Stacy's eyes blazed with anger. She pointed her weapon at Melissa and pulled the trigger. Melissa jumped as a crossbow bolt buried itself in the wall beside her.

"Jesus!" Melissa yelled.

"Why are you doing this?" Jason yelled, suddenly very aware of the danger they were both in.

"Because I'm done with it, Jason," Stacy said, pointing her crossbow back at him, "I'm done with being in last place. I'm sick and tired of being talked down to and coddled and held back while the rest of you save the world."

"What?" Melissa said incredulously. "You're mad because you feel like we're better than you?"

"I'm mad because you know that you're better than me," Stacy replied, "and you show it every damn chance you get. I can't do the things you do. I can't run on top of cars or beat up twelve people at once or punch through a wall. I can't do that. I can't do anything!"

"Stacy," Jason said calmly, "you know that's not true. You've helped us more than once. You probably saved my life when I fought Raven the day you all came to rescue me, and you didn't even know me yet."

"I knew we should have left you behind," Melissa said angrily.

"Dammit, Melissa!" Jason yelled.

Stacy stomped forward, bringing her weapon to bear and pointing it inches from Melissa's forehead.

"You hated me from day one, didn't you? You arrogant bitch. I looked up to you like a sister, and all you ever wanted was to use me and then get rid of me so you could have the men all to yourself."

She then spun around and walked back to the other end of the room. They could see her chest hitching as she walked. Stacy was crying.

Jason leaned towards Melissa.

"Did you see that?" he whispered.

"I know, she's crazy. She's crying now," Melissa answered.

"No," Jason said, "her crossbow. It had another bolt in it when she pointed it at you. Did you see her reload?"

Melissa thought for a moment. No. Stacy hadn't placed another bolt after shooting the first one at the wall - and yet the weapon had been loaded when it was pointed at her just now.

"Something weird's going on here," Jason said.

"You think?" Melissa said back.

Stacy spun back around, pointing her weapon at Melissa again.

"Maybe you are better than me, Melissa. Maybe you're prettier and stronger and funnier than me. Maybe everybody likes you better. BUT I'M THE ONE WITH THE DAMN CROSSBOW POINTED AT YOUR HEAD!!!"

Melissa sat back, shocked by the ferocity of Stacy's words and the sheer anguish in her eyes.

"We're your friends, Stacy. Whatever's happening, we'll help you get through it," Jason said.

"You shut up," Stacy said, pointing the weapon at him. "You're no one's friend, Jason. We saved your life, gave you a place to stay, and what do you care about? Sure as hell not us. All you care about is finding your damn mother and killing Raven. You'd leave us in a heartbeat if you had a chance to do either of those, wouldn't you?"

Jason said nothing.

"WOULDN'T YOU?!!!" she screamed.

"Yes!" Jason shouted back.

Melissa looked at him.

"Yes," he repeated. "You're exactly right, Stacy. I would. If the three of you hadn't been there that day, I would have gotten myself out. I would have killed Raven. I would be out there looking for my mother. Maybe I would have found her already. So you want me to say that I think you're all just holding me back? Fine. You're right. I do think that."

Stacy seemed caught off guard.

"Sometimes I wish I wasn't here. Sometimes I think the right thing to do is to devote all of my time and energy to finding my mom, but you know what? I stay here anyway. I stay here because I owe all of you. You fought for me. I may not want to be here sometimes, but I don't put a damn weapon to your head because of it!"

There was a moment of silence between them. Stacy seemed unsure of what to say next. Finally, she broke the silence.

"What do you think of that, Melissa? Your boyfriend thinks he'd be better off without you."

Melissa looked long and hard at Jason.

"Maybe he's right," she said softly.

"Melissa…" Jason said. "That's not what I meant."

"But it is, Jason," Stacy said. "And Melissa, you don't need us either. Neither does Nick. You're all a bunch of selfish loners. You don't need each other at all."

"But you need us, don't you, Stacy?" came Nick's voice from behind her.

She spun around to see him standing there, silently walking up the last step to the attic. His clothes were dirty and torn. She could see blood seeping through in a couple of places.

For a moment her weapon drooped in her hands and her eyes showed nothing but concern. But then as Nick came closer, the fire came back into her eyes and she raised her crossbow towards him again.

Nick could see that there really was something in her eyes. Her deep brown eyes were laced with a kind of red undertone. He wouldn't have seen it if he weren't standing this close to her.

"You're exactly right," Nick said. "We are all loners. Jason cares most about revenge. Until recently, Melissa only really cared about punishing the people that hurt her. And I only care about this stupid Pull inside of me. I'm no different from Jason. Sometimes I think I shouldn't be here with you either."

He took a step closer.

"But you're different, aren't you, Stacy?"

She took a step back, glaring at him angrily and continuing to show him the threat of her weapon held just two feet now from his head.

"You actually need us. You don't have a grand quest to undertake. No revenge against someone who hurt you. No hidden memories to discover. No great battle to fight. All you want is a family. All you want is us."

"But you don't need me!" she said, half screaming and half sobbing. "None of you do!"

"You know what, Stacy? The fact that there isn't some great burden on your shoulders…the fact that you want nothing more than to be right here…that's exactly why we need you. Because you're right - Melissa, Jason and I are loners. We're incomplete people. If we were off on our own, sure we'd be walking our own paths, but we'd also be spiraling towards self-destruction."

Melissa and Jason listened intently, feeling the truth of Nick's words as he spoke them.

"All three of us are lost. As strong as we may be…we're still too weak to stand alone for long. We're like pieces of debris floating in a great wide abyss, waiting to get swallowed up. But you…" Nick said, taking a step closer, "you are the chain that holds us together."

Her eyes were showing nothing but tears now. Her shoulders slumped and her weapon drooped but remained pointed at Nick's chest.

"In a way, you're the strongest one of us. We need that. We need your laugh. We need your compassion. We need your hope. That's why we love you, Stacy."

He took the final step towards her, letting the tip of her crossbow bolt poke directly into his chest.

"That's why I love you."

With that, Stacy let out a great sob and let her weapon clatter to the floor. She fell forward into Nick's arms.

"This isn't you," Nick said to her. "I know this isn't you. Now come back to us."

"I'm trying, Nick. I'm trying but it's so hard," she said. She seemed on the verge of passing out.

"We're with you, Stacy," Jason said. He turned to Melissa and nudged her in the arm.

She looked at him defiantly. But Jason held her gaze just and strongly. He was telling her wordlessly to forgive their friend.

"Something did this to her," Nick said. "I think it was The Whisper. I think he got inside of her like he did me."

Melissa looked at him.

"The dreams?" she said, suddenly seeing a pattern emerging.

"I'm so sorry," Stacy said. She seemed half asleep. She leaned limp into Nick's arms.

"Shut up, Stacy," Melissa said. "Shut up and fight it."

Stacy heard those words and then was out. She drifted into unconsciousness in Nick's arms, but instead of slipping into the muffled embrace of sleep, she seemed almost to wake up somewhere else entirely.

Nick was right. She had been feeling it, like an itch in the back of her skull, for weeks now. Every bad thought, every angry sentiment, every time one of them would say something and she would take offense to it…she felt as though there was something inside, prodding those feelings on.

It started with her dreams. Dreams she could still not fully remember. They were images, she thought. Images of her friends betraying her - leaving her behind or blaming her for things going wrong. Every happy thought was attacked in those dreams. Every pleasure at having finally found people who truly needed her came under assault by something.

Someone.

She was standing in the yard of a small house now. She could tell it was a blue house with red shutters, but she paid little attention to the details of her surroundings.

Her eyes were locked on the dark figure in the doorway.

"Hello, Stacy," the figure spoke

When it spoke, Stacy's world fell apart. Her heart collapsed inside of her. Her mind turned in on itself in an attempt to hide from the implications of that voice. That cold, familiar voice.

It was not The Whisper that attacked her.

What stood before her was something infinitely more terrible.

Nick lay beside Stacy on her bed, holding her hand and watching the rise and fall of her chest and the back and forth roll of her closed eyes. Eyes that told them she was dreaming again.

Melissa and Jason sat at the foot of the bed, watching her as well. Blitz was also on the bed, curled up beside Stacy's legs.

"What do you think's going to happen, Nick?" Jason asked him.

"She's fighting him, I think. She'll force him out, like I did."

"So that's why he wants you so bad?" Melissa said, rubbing her sore wrists. "Because he tried to...whatever...eat your mind? And you forced him out?"

"Something like that," Nick replied.

"So all those things she said - everything that's been happening with her lately...wasn't really her?" she asked, still confused.

"No," Jason said. "There was part of her up there. She meant everything she said. I just don't think she really meant the malice behind it."

"Hmm," Melissa looked at Stacy, uncertain. "Well, I guess this makes more sense than Miss Giggle Puffs turning into...what we saw upstairs."

"Nothing makes sense anymore," Jason sighed. "But Nick's right. We have to stick together in times like this. Stacy's one of us, no matter what she's done or what she truly feels."

They both looked at Nick. He seemed to be only partially aware that they were there. His eyes and his attention were focused only on her.

After a few more minutes, Stacy began to stir. She opened her eyes and looked at Nick.

For a second, perhaps two, Melissa and Jason thought they saw fear in her eyes as she looked at him. Her body went rigid and her right hand gripped the bed as if preparing to pull herself away.

But then she relaxed. They saw her hand let go of the sheets and the fear leave her eyes. They had a strange sensation that she had just forced herself to not be afraid.

She rolled towards Nick and wrapped her arms around him. She pulled him towards her and held him tightly.

"It's over," she said. "He's gone."

Nick smiled and held her back just as fiercely.

"Welcome back," he said.

She let him go and sat up, facing Melissa and Jason.

"I'm sorry I hurt you both. I'm sorry for the things I said. It wasn't all me, but part of it was. If you can't forgive me…"

"Shut the hell up, girl," Melissa said. She grabbed Stacy's arms and pulled her towards her, wrapping her in a big hug.

"I know you better than you think," Melissa said, "and I know you never would have really hurt us."

Jason thought she was right. Stacy probably would have turned her crossbow upon herself before shooting any of them.

Stacy gripped Melissa back, laughing and letting tears fall from her eyes.

"Thank you so much," she said to Melissa.

"Thank all of you."

17

The following day carried a sense that it should have been awkward - that Stacy's rampage should have left them all with a sense of dread and mistrust. Instead, what followed was almost a feeling of cleansing. Of rebirth. As if they had passed a test. Emotionally, the strongest of them had come under assault. And, though she had faltered, in the end she had won.

Stacy and Jason sat on the back porch overlooking the lake, both rocking back and forth with mugs of hot cocoa. The weather was beginning to get rather cold. Winter was almost upon them in full force.

"Nick's on a crusade now," Jason said. "He's convinced that we have no choice but to kill The Whisper."

Stacy nodded, taking a sip of her cocoa.

"Melissa's right beside him. She's been itching to really try herself against that thing for a while now."

Again, Stacy nodded.

"Do you think we can beat it?" he asked her directly.

She seemed to think for a moment but then finally shook her head.

"I don't see how. But he's right that we have to try. If we don't...he'll keep following us everywhere we go."

"But you were able to beat him," Jason said, "in your head. That's what you did last night, right?"

Jason studied her while awaiting her answer. Ever since last night he had the sensation that she was not telling them the whole truth about what had really happened to her.

Stacy just nodded, looking down at her drink.

"Stacy, he's really gone, isn't he?"

She looked up at him and smiled genuinely.

"Yes. It's a little...difficult to talk about exactly what happened right now, but I promise you he's gone. I beat him last night. He won't try something like that again - not with me, at least."

153

Jason seemed satisfied. For, whatever she was hiding, he did not believe that Stacy was lying to him.

"I'm glad you're back, Stace. I know you were right there with us, but I don't think it's inaccurate to say that we all missed you these last few weeks."

She smiled and reached out to take hold of his hand.

"I was there, Jason. During the tough times, that was mostly me. David, the bounty hunters, what happened with your brother. I was there - just…different."

"When do you think it started?" he asked.

"The night before you and Melissa left for Alabama," she answered, "I remember feeling different after that night. And then Nick and I had our little…tussle…and I think it just kicked into high gear. Whatever insecurity I was feeling…it let that thing in like an open door."

Jason sat back and looked out over the lake.

"Demons that feed on insecurity," he said. "What a strange world I find myself in these days."

She smiled.

"No kidding. Just a year and a half ago, the most amazing thing I had to look forward to was an old beat-up copy of The Lion, The Witch and The Wardrobe."

"Hmph. I guess it does kind of feel like we all stepped into Narnia somehow," he said pensively.

"I get the feeling though," she said. "that all we had before…all the normal things and uneventful days…those were just a prequel to this. Our lives before we came together…they were just a preparation for what we're living now."

Jason looked at her.

"You're saying this is all fate?"

She shrugged.

"Maybe. But for all the strange things that have happened to us, doesn't it all feel right? I know you want to be looking for your mom, but being here…doesn't it feel perfectly natural? Like this is always where you were meant to be?"

Jason looked back at the lake. He nodded slowly.

"Yeah. Now that I think about it, sometimes it does."

They both stared at the lake for a while, thinking about Stacy's words, and how right it felt to be here, with each other. With Nick and Melissa and Blitz. Living every day knowing it was them against the world.

"I can't call it fate, though," Jason said. "I'm too much of a man of reason. But you're right, Stace. However we got here...it was right for all of us."

She looked at him.

"You don't blame me at all for what happened, do you?" she said, looking at the bruise she had left on his forehead.

Jason shook his head.

"Stacy, with all the hate I keep bottled up...with all the blame I hold for Jacob...I'm the last person that can blame anyone for feeling angry."

"Even though I hurt you?" she said.

He nodded, "I look at myself in the mirror sometimes - at what I've become...and I wonder if I might not be capable of the same thing someday."

Her eyes filled with concern.

"We won't let that happen."

He smiled,and took her hand this time.

"I know you won't," he said.

"Melissa doesn't blame you either," he then said, changing the subject. "She's definitely one to hold a grudge - but it was you, Stacy. I don't think any of us could hate you if we tried."

Stacy felt her eyes tear up. They all had been making her feel so loved, despite what she had done.

"And Nick worships the ground you walk on," he said. "You could cut off both his arms and he'd still love you."

She let go of his hand and sighed.

"But that's not enough," she said, not with sadness, but with understanding.

Jason shook his head.

"No. That one's got too many issues. Too many hang-ups. I think he'll work through them some day - maybe when he's done with The Whisper and that Pull of his. But in the meantime, you'll just have to be satisfied knowing how he really feels about you."

She smiled.

"I am."

Jason smiled, too. He knew that she meant it. She wasn't worried anymore. She didn't blame him anymore. She loved Nick back, he thought, from whatever distance she had to.

"Stacy," he said, "last night, when we were up in the attic...Melissa and I saw something."

She turned to him, suddenly worried about the turn of the conversation.

"You didn't reload your crossbow after you shot it into the wall. We didn't see it happen, but another bolt was just…there."

She looked away. Jason could see the confusion on her face.

"I…didn't even realize," she said.

"It wasn't the demon. I know because it's happened to me, too," he said.

She looked at him in surprise.

"I was in the gym the other day, on the heavy bag. I was thinking about Raven, and hitting it as hard and as fast as I could. The next thing I knew, there was this sensation of…letting go…and then my fist went through the bag."

Her eyes widened.

"Completely through it," he said. "That shouldn't be possible."

She looked down at the floor and began chewing nervously on her fingernail, her eyes distant.

"So you think that thing with the crossbow was really…me?" she asked.

"Yes," he replied, "I think we're changing."

She nodded slowly. There had been times during battle, or when she was target shooting in the gym, that Stacy had felt almost…euphoric. She had felt as if she were dancing on the edge of limitation, and that if she let go just a little bit….

"Melissa and Nick fought on top of a moving truck," he said. "How is that possible?"

"But Nick's always done things like that," she said and then looked up at him in realization.

"You think it's him?"

Jason nodded.

"I don't know how or why, but I think the longer we're around him, the more we become like him. Physical limitations don't seem to exist for him. Melissa's getting more and more like that, too, but she doesn't think about it. I think that's part of why she's so good. She doesn't stop to think about what she can't do."

"He's pressing the boundaries," she said, "and now we are too."

"Whatever he is, he's powerful. David knew that. The Whisper knows it. Maybe the bounty hunters know it, too. Hell, maybe they're already like him. Like us."

She nodded.

"I think so. Byron moved faster than any person should be able to."

She looked up at him.

"So what do you think this means?"

He smiled a bit.

"I think it means we should actually try to push it next time. See what we can get away with. And," he said. "I think it means we might actually stand a chance against The Whisper."

She smiled, possibility dawning on her face.

"We might actually have a shot at ending this," she said.

Jason sat back and nodded.

"Him, at least. And that's a pretty big step forward. Not just for Nick, but for all of us."

Stacy looked out at the lake, her mind and her heart suddenly filling with hope.

Nick called them all into the living room that evening. They could see on his face that he meant business. His arms were crossed and he stood in front of the television, facing them as they sat down.

"Tonight, we're going to kill The Whisper," he said, getting right to the point.

"Whoa," Melissa said, "right to the 'we.' I don't even have to fight you on this?"

Nick shook his head.

"Not this time. That monster hurt one of our own. We all get a shot at him, no matter how dangerous."

"Damn, Nick," Jason said, "it's about time you put on your big boy pants and realized you can't take on the world by yourself."

"If I had stood against David alone, like I wanted to, I'd be dead," Nick said, looking at Melissa, who nodded at him approvingly.

"Besides," Nick said. "I told you all about my confrontation with The Whisper Halloween night. He wiped the floor with me. I'm no match for him by myself."

"Nick..." Stacy said. "We don't have to do this."

He looked at her, seeming surprised.

"If we don't, Stacy, he'll keep trying to hurt us, from without and within. He's too dangerous and too much of a threat. If we ever want to live normal lives…The Whisper has to die."

157

They all took those words in, not for a moment doubting the truth of them.

"But what makes you think we even can kill him?" Melissa asked. "Jason and I saw that thing get run over by a sixteen-wheeler. He seems more or less invincible."

"To anything conventional," Jason said. "But the four of us are anything but."

They all looked at him.

"Stacy can fire her crossbow without reloading it. You saw that too, Melissa. I can punch through a heavy-bag and…there are times when I think I may have…altered the trajectory of my chain just by thinking about it."

"Jason," Stacy said, "you didn't tell me that."

"I can't prove it yet," he said. "It's just a feeling I've had."

"So you're saying we all have super powers?" Melissa asked.

"Melissa, you were fighting on top of a speeding truck right next to Nick the other day," Jason answered. "You've always been amazingly fast and incredibly strong, but lately you seem to be getting even faster and stronger. The emotion you fuel into combat makes you a force of nature."

She looked at the coffee table. They could all see in her eyes that she didn't completely disagree with Jason's words.

"It's true. I do kick ass," she said. "But this is still surprising coming from you Jason. You've always been the reasonable one of the group."

"I still am," he said. "I believe things when I see them. And you've all been seeing the same crazy shit I've been seeing for over a year now. You want a good example?"

Jason looked at Blitz.

"Blitz, guard the door. I think Raven's outside."

The dog immediately sprang out from under the coffee table, ran to the door, and began growling with his haunches raised. The rest of them watched in surprise.

"It's okay, Blitz. False alarm. We're safe," Jason said.

Blitz turned to look at him and looked back nervously at the door before trotting back over and sitting down at Nick's feet. His eyes still seemed cautious and alert, however.

"See?" Jason said. "Even the dog's different."

"Different…" Nick said thoughtfully.

They all looked at him.

"And then there's him," Melissa said.

"The strangest of all of us," Jason agreed.

"No," Stacy said sternly. "I don't care what he can do. I don't care how he's changed us. Nick is no different from anyone else. He's flesh and blood just like the rest of us."

They all looked at her, including Nick.

He smiled at her thankfully and then glanced over at Jason. "You really think I'm...changing you?"

Jason nodded.

"Something is, Nick. All five of us can do things that shouldn't be possible. And we're only getting better at it. It started when we met you. If it isn't you...it's something that followed you - some force that's been opening our eyes to something."

Stacy gripped the couch as he said those last words, hoping the others didn't notice.

Melissa stared off into the distance. For her, Jason's words weren't entirely true. Meeting Nick had not been the trigger factor in her...change. No, that had happened long before.

Nick thought of The Pull. It was obvious to him now that The Pull wasn't just some memory or instinctual yearning. No, he recognized now that it was the calling of an external force - a voice speaking from the pit of his soul. He believed it was connected to the little girl. She and The Pull represented something that was drawing him forward towards some great purpose. It wasn't altogether unreasonable to think that same force might bolster the strength of his friends as well.

"Okay," Nick finally said, breaking the reflective silence. "Then we really have a shot at beating him."

"Damn straight," Melissa said. "I'll just go all Wonder Woman on his metal ass."

"So, now that we've established that," Jason said. "You called this meeting, Nick. What's the plan?"

Nick looked up, the resolve back in his eyes.

"We take the fight to him for once."

"I like the sound of that," Melissa said.

"You would," Stacy said, giving her a good-natured poke. "The thought of violence makes you drool like a fat kid in a candy store."

"Hey, fat kids can be cool, too," Melissa responded.

159

"We find an empty lot. A construction site that's well lit, or a parking lot. Something with lots of open ground and room to maneuver. We bring Blitz as an alarm system. He always runs away when The Whisper's close. That will cut out his advantage of surprise."

"It's okay, Blitz. Everyone knows you're brave," Stacy said, reaching over and stroking the dog's head.

Blitz wagged his tail happily, but kept his eyes locked on Nick, as if he were listening with the rest of them.

"And then," Nick said, "we hit him as a team. We throw everything we've got at him. If there's a way to bring him down permanently, we'll find it."

"Punches and kicks won't be enough to take that thing out," Jason said. "Got a secret weapon in mind?"

Nick smiled.

"I have a couple of ideas," he said coyly.

18

"You know, you're basing this whole thing on a pretty big assumption. What the hell happens if your 'idea' doesn't work?" Jason asked as they stood in the nearly vacant parking lot that night, preparing themselves for what was to come.

"It'll work," Nick said. "It has to."

Before arriving at the lot for their fated battle, the five of them had made a short stop. Nick had entered, alone, into a cathedral outside of the city. He walked in wearing full Hero regalia, mask and all. He strode right up to a priest and asked unashamedly for his sword to be blessed.

From what he told the others, the priest had only hesitated momentarily. He then performed the rights upon the weapon and upon Nick himself. Apparently, Nick said, the priest had been a fan.

So here they were, taking a leap of faith, ready to fight a monster with nothing but determination, a religiously empowered weapon, and their own possibly supernatural skills to rely on.

The five positioned themselves under a streetlight, facing towards the dark wooded lot that adjoined the parking area they had chosen. Nick stood in the center with Blitz at his heel. Melissa stood to one side of him and Jason to another. Stacy stood behind, her back to a short brick wall, with her crossbow cocked and ready. She had brought a secret weapon of her own. Byron's rapier was strapped to her hip. She had been practicing with it on occasion since he had given it to her. None of them would be defenseless this evening, and all were ready to fight to the end.

They would stamp out their greatest threat, or die trying.

"It won't be long," Nick said. "He's been following us. He always is."

The others said nothing and only listened to the soundless winter night and the drumbeat of their own nervous hearts.

"Somebody's gonna lose an eye tonight, I just know it," Melissa said.

"Don't jinx us, M," Jason admonished her, though he secretly believed she was probably right. It was unlikely they would walk away from this in one piece, if they walked away at all.

Nick stared out into the darkness.

"You want us so bad?" Nick yelled into the night. "Here we are. We're all ready for you. I'm calling you out, Whisper! We can beat you, and we're going to prove it. Right here, right now."

All of them fell silent then, listening and only half hoping that Nick's summons would be answered. The other half was absolutely terrified that it would.

Moments of silence passed. They began to believe that it had all been for nothing, that they could all go home and enjoy another uneventful night.

But then Blitz suddenly yelped and ran off into the darkness.

Their alarm had sounded. The summons had been answered. The Whisper had arrived.

He strode confidently into view in front of them, his illuminated grin emerging from the darkness followed by the reflection of the streetlight off of his metal form. As he walked, his bladed hands swung casually beside him, nearly long enough to scrape the pavement.

He paused twenty feet from them and seemed to take them in.

"Can't stay away, can you?" Nick taunted.

The Whisper regarded him with what seemed like amusement.

"Shit," Melissa muttered beneath her breath with a mixture of fear and anticipation. "C'mon, shit, shit, shit, shit."

"We're ready for this," Stacy said from behind her. "Remember what we practiced."

"This time we're challenging you!" Nick announced, bringing his sword to bear. "This time it's on our ground. Our rules."

The Whisper's eyes gleamed, both figuratively and literally. His smiled widened.

They knew the challenge had been accepted.

With an ethereal hiss, The Whisper scraped his claws together, whipped his arms to his side, then charged.

Nick roared a furious battle cry and entered into a charge of his own.

"Kill or be killed, guys!" Melissa yelled. "Let's kick some ass!"

When Nick and The Whisper met, steel to unearthly steel, the clash rang out like a cosmic wrecking ball.

Nick jumped forward, determined to land the first strike. The Whisper brought his hands to bear, shielding his face from Nick's assault. Nick landed on the monster's chest, his sword slamming down into The Whisper's defenses.

The monster cringed, and for an instant, Nick felt hope.

But then his smiled flashed brighter, and he thrust his arms outward, flinging Nick away like an unwanted parasite.

Melissa ran forward even as Nick flew above her. She darted into the monster's spread arms like projectile shot from a cannon, spinning in the air and thrusting her staff at The Whisper's grinning face. Her weapon connected with a smack, and she heard the monster scream in surprise.

Jason circled around the beast, waiting for the correct opening to play his role. The eyes beneath his shades watched those bladed arms as they flailed at Melissa.

Melissa sidestepped and deflected one strike, then another. She kicked at the monster's knee, a blow that would have sent any man crashing to the ground. Instead, she heard the sound of her own foot fracturing as it collided with the unyielding metal.

She cried out in pain, and The Whisper came forward with a downward swipe at her neck.

His arm halted in midair as Jason's chain wrapped around his wrist.

His head then rocked violently as four bolts from Stacy's crossbow thudded forcefully into his eye sockets.

Four bolts in two seconds. So Stacy had found her groove, Jason thought.

And then, to Jason's amazement, Nick jumped from above him, landed on his outstretched chain, and ran along it like a tightrope, leaping near the end and landing a flipping slash to the back of The Whisper's head.

There could be no more doubt. Tonight, they all fought like heroes.

The Whisper roared, whipping his arm around and loosing himself from Jason's chain. He took another blow from Nick to his back, then knocked Melissa's staff to the side and kicked her in the chest.

The others heard her exhale violently as the wind was forced from her lungs. She flew back a few feet and landed roughly on her behind.

Nick jumped on The Whisper's shoulders and began hammering away with his sword.

Jason and Stacy decided to close the distance, maintaining the momentum of their assault while Melissa regained her strength. Stacy drew her sword and ran forward while Jason looped his weapon around his fist with unnatural speed and charged into the frantic beast, landing a vicious left hook with his metal-clad hand.

The Whisper began moving faster and more erratically, obviously unused to being on the defensive. It reached a finger above its head, spearing Nick in the back. Nick yelled and fell from his enemy's shoulders. The Whisper then slashed at Jason. Jason jumped back, but suffered two deep cuts in his ribs.

Instead of backing off, however, Jason only pushed forward, throwing another punch at the demon, which this time was dodged. The Whisper glared at him. Jason knew that their enemy meant business. Play time was over.

Stacy slashed at the thing's hands twice with her rapier and then thrust forward, jabbing at its chest, hoping to chance upon a weak point. The weapon only slid off of the metal exterior. The Whisper slashed again at Jason while bringing his face forward to roar menacingly at Stacy.

She did not relent under the ferocity of the gesture. Instead, she brought her crossbow to bear in her left hand and shot another bolt into the thing's mouth.

"Make a hole!" Melissa yelled, jumping back into the fray, bringing her staff slamming down onto The Whisper's head.

Nick struggled to his feet and watched his friends engaged in the deadliest of dances with his mortal enemy. Together, they were keeping The Whisper on the defensive, and that was no small victory. It was not enough, however. Eventually they would tire, and then the monster would carve them to pieces. Something drastic had to be done, and it had to happen soon.

"Time to bring down the elephant!" Nick yelled, sounding out the code phrase for the last-ditch maneuver they had practiced earlier.

"Oh shit, here we go," Melissa said, moving around The Whisper as carefully as she could.

Stacy and Jason backed off. She leveled her crossbow while Jason let the chain fall from his wrist again.

Nick ran back in front of the beast.

The Whisper stood there, weapons bared and chest heaving. Not with any need to breathe, they all knew, but likely with the sheer joy and battle lust they could see reflecting from its unnaturally expressive, flaming eyes.

"Now you go down," Nick said and charged forward once more.

Jason sprang into motion, flinging his chain around The Whisper's neck.

As The Whisper grasped at the chain, Stacy sent a powerful shot into the beast's midsection, knocking its center of gravity back and making it double over slightly.

Behind The Whisper, Melissa was also charging forward.

Jason jerked his chain, further bringing the beast off balance.

And then Melissa jumped and Nick skid to the ground, flipping onto his hands and spinning his lower body, both legs whipping around like a propeller.

With a thundering kick, Melissa hit The Whisper in the back of the skull. Simultaneously, Nick spun underneath his enemy, knocking the legs out from under him.

For an instant, The Whisper was completely horizontal in the air - with Nick whirling by underneath him and Melissa sailing by above.

And when that instant was over, The Whisper's head smacked into the asphalt with enough force to rattle the windows of the cars on the other side of the lot. A loud boom echoed out as his metal skull dug a small crater into the pavement below.

Nick and Melissa got back to their feet, and all of them backed up, their eyes locked on their fallen enemy in anticipation.

His face buried in the asphalt, The Whisper did not move.

"Did we do it?" Melissa asked, breathing heavily.

Nick said nothing, his posture still at the ready.

"That should have killed anything," Jason said, hopefully but cautiously.

They continued to watch for several more seconds as their enemy lay spread-eagle on the pavement.

And then his arms moved at his sides and he pushed down, attempting to pull his buried head from the ground.

"No," Stacy said with defeat in her voice.

"No," Nick echoed. "No!"

He ran forward, an angry gleam in his eyes.

"Melissa!" he yelled as he ran. "Give me a boost! Now!"

The Whisper succeeded in yanking his head free, and they could now see that he was smiling more gleefully than ever.

Melissa didn't think. She swung her staff as Nick ran by. She did not question as Nick jumped upon the tip of her weapon. None of them did. Neither did they question when she successfully hurled him like a projectile from the end of it.

"Die!" Nick screamed as he rocketed forward, his sword aimed downwards at his enemy's heart.

He hit The Whisper with the force of a missile, the tip of his weapon gouging into the demon's metal flesh.

The Whisper stood, catching Nick, but not fast enough to stop the sword from colliding with his chest. The demon stood his ground, despite the ferocity of the attack. This time, his feet buried themselves into the pavement with the momentum of Nick's assault.

Stacy, Jason and Melissa watched expectantly, desperately hoping that Nick's blessed sword had pierced The Whisper's shell.

Nick looked as well....and saw that it had not.

The Whisper gave a raspy laugh, and looked at Nick with its taunting eyes.

"Too weak," it said, in a voice only Nick heard.

Nick screamed in frustration and jumped off of The Whisper, slashing several times before landing a few feet away. He immediately sprang back at his enemy, slashing furiously, yelling like a madman as he did.

The Whisper laughed as Nick screamed, and began parrying and countering Nick's strikes with slashes of its own.

"God, what do we do now?" Melissa said, feeling defeated and helpless.

"I...I don't know," Jason said, having no back-up plan at all. It had been all or nothing. They had known how slim a chance it was to be able to take The Whisper down, but they had all had so much faith in their abilities that they did not let themselves pause to contemplate the possibility of defeat. And now here that defeat was, grinning spitefully in their faces.

Suddenly Stacy's roar rang out, joining Nick's in its echo across the parking lot. She shot several bolts at The Whisper. Each one bounced off harmlessly, but she did not relent, and soon several more were in the air.

Jason and Melissa could see it plain as day now. Each time a bolt was fired from her weapon, another would just appear in its place. Nor did she need to pause to cock the crossbow. Through sheer willpower, she could now fire her bow like an automatic weapon.

"Fuck it," Melissa said, running to join Nick in his futile attack.

Nick struck, he dodged, and he moved, but each blow he landed simply bounced off. The Whisper, on the other hand, was adding several deep cuts and lacerations to Nick's sides, chest, and legs, joining the deep wound on his back.

Nick cried out in pain and anger, once more bringing his sword down on The Whisper's arm with no effect.

Melissa joined in as well, hammering her staff into the thing's neck and ribs. The Whisper, however, seemed to pay her no mind. It was focused solely on Nick.

The Whisper swiped forward, cutting through Nick's weakening defenses with ease and digging four bladed fingers deep into his ribcage.

Nick whimpered and stumbled back, holding his sword in front of him more like a scrawny child than a hardened warrior. Tears of rage fell down his cheeks, soaking into his mask.

Melissa screamed and hammered again and again into The Whisper's back, trying to get his attention off of Nick, to no avail.

The Whisper jumped into the air, landing on Nick with a painful thump.

"This," The Whisper spoke to him while a taloned foot dug into his stomach and a finger sliced playfully into his neck, "never ends."

Nick let his sword clatter to the ground and his head fall back onto the pavement.

Melissa charged into The Whisper's side. The Whisper snarled and stood up, picking her up like a toy.

It roared into her face and then hurled her like a football across the parking lot.

Jason and Stacy watched as Melissa sailed high into the air, finally coming down with a crash on the hood of a parked car.

167

Jason ran off towards her. Stacy looked back towards the demon, preparing herself for it to come after her next.

Instead, it was standing over Nick again. It picked him up and brought the boy to its face. Nick was just as emotionally beaten as he was physically, and Stacy suddenly realized with terror that he would not fight back.

"Which one of them dies tonight?"

"Please don't" Nick pleaded. "Please just kill me."

"Which one?" it asked again.

"Just…KILL ME!!!" Nick screamed in impotent rage.

For a moment, Stacy thought The Whisper would do just that. But then she heard something behind her. The rush of something approaching fast.

Blitz.

The dog raced past her, moving at a speed she had never seen him move before. His teeth were bared, but he did not make a sound.

The Whisper was too focused on Nick. It didn't see the angry projectile racing towards it.

"Which o…"

"No!" Stacy screamed, knowing her voice would not stop the dog in his mission to protect his best friend.

Blitz jumped into the air, right at The Whisper's face.

The demon noticed the dog at the last second, and at that last second he let Nick go and thrust a bladed hand out to deflect the dog's assault.

Nick lay there, looking up at his hated enemy and his truest friend, suddenly locked in what looked like a mad embrace. The Whisper struggled as Blitz snapped repeatedly at its face, his paws peddling and pushing The Whisper's chest.

On its face, Nick could see an expression he wasn't used to seeing on the metal demon: pure shock.

But then Nick noticed something else. The Whisper wasn't holding the dog so much as trying to shake the dog free. He could not.

He could not because Blitz was impaled on one of his blades.

Nick jumped to his feet, and as he did so the demon finally managed to fling Blitz off of him. Still snarling, Blitz flew through the air and landed with a thump several feet away.

Nick didn't see it, his eyes so focused on his fallen friend, but Stacy saw The Whisper stare at the dog in surprise for a moment longer before running off into the night. The monster had what it had wanted, though it had not come the way it intended. The Whisper had won.

Blitz struggled to get back to his feet as Nick arrived at his side. He grabbed the dog, forcing him to remain still.

Nick felt warm blood coat his shirt as he held his friend.

Stacy ran to them. In the distance, the car Melissa had landed on was sounding an alarm, but she did not notice, nor did she notice Jason holding Melissa up as they hobbled from behind the vehicle.

"Oh no," Jason said with heartbreaking disappointment when he saw the scene in front of them.

Nick held Blitz in his arms and Stacy sat beside them. The dog struggled a bit as if still believing they were in danger.

"It's okay. It's okay. He's gone now. You got him for me," Nick said softly.

Blitz seemed to relax a bit at the sound of Nick's voice. He stopped struggling and allowed Nick to hold him.

Stacy couldn't see the wound, but she did see the blood. It was covering Nick and pooling up on the pavement below them. This wasn't like the time The Whisper had cut her and left her bleeding. No, this was much, much worse.

Nick felt a warm, wet tongue lick his face. He smiled.

"You were so brave," he told the dog, genuinely proud of him.

Blitz licked him again.

"Nick, we need to get him to a clinic," Jason said. He and Melissa were now standing over them.

Nick nodded. He picked the dog up and the four of them hurried to their car in the next lot. Jason had expected wounds and had already covered the back seat with blankets to soak up any blood. None of them had expected this much of it.

"You saved me tonight, buddy," Nick said. Jason started up the car and pulled out onto the road. Stacy was in the back seat with them and Melissa was in the front seat, the pain of her own wounds completely forgotten. Jason looked over at her once and saw her eyes watering and her lip quivering.

"You saved me," Nick said again, clutching the dog as tight as he could.

About five minutes into the drive, Stacy noticed that Blitz's chest was no longer rising and falling. His head was nuzzled by Nick's neck, but he was very still.

She reached forward and put a hand on Jason's shoulder.

He pulled the car over, and they sat there by the side of the road.

Nick offered no protest. He knew his friend was gone.

"Please," he wept. "Please don't leave me,"

Stacy stared out the window. She couldn't bear to look at them.

"Please don't leave me."

19

Nick buried Blitz in the front yard of the lake house. They had offered to help, but he insisted on doing it himself. He said it had just been the two of them at the beginning and it should be just the two of them at the end.

Stacy was with him now, sitting behind him with her arms wrapped around his back as he sat there, staring at the grave. Melissa didn't like the look in his eyes. It was as much a look of resignation as one of sorrow.

"My God," she said as the two of them stood on the front porch, watching two of their friends sit by the grave of a third. "This has got to be...."

"One of the hardest night's of your life?" Jason finished for her.

She nodded.

To think that she would never see Nick's furry little shadow follow him in the door after a night of wandering again. That she would never hear those paws clomp up the stairs to find her or Stacy or Jason when Nick wasn't there and jump up on their bed for a nap. That she would never see the dog in battle again, so fierce and fearless. Truly fearless, she realized, as he had conquered his last fear in one selfless act to protect his best friend.

A fresh wave of tears threatened to overcome her. She wiped her arm under her nose and Jason put his arm around her.

"How do we do it, Jason?" she asked. "How do we keep fighting something that can do this to us?"

"We can't let this stop us," Jason said. "If we do, that thing will have won."

"It did win," she said.

"No," he said. "We'll find a way."

Thomas Cross sat at his desk late that night, staring at a registry he'd been studying for hours. Several files were opened in front of him, all nearly empty, on people society had nearly forgotten.

Jason Dreddowski, Stacy Cross - two nobodies with no criminal record, though Stacy at least had a military record thanks to her father enrolling her in instructional courses with the ROTC. Flight training. Minor hand-to-hand combat. Marksmanship. Jason was just a street kid, notable only for his disappearance and subsequent reappearance. His mother's whereabouts were still unknown.

Melissa Lunar Moonbeam did, in fact, have a sizable criminal record. A number of assault charges - petty thievery, drunk and disorderly, resisting arrest. Not to mention the fact that she was technically a runaway, though her father never reported her. Formerly employed by RavenCorp before reportedly being terminated early last year.

These files had led him nowhere. So, in a moment of inspiration, Detective Cross turned to the missing persons directory.

"Bingo," he said, stopping on a single file among an endless list of them

Male Caucasian - brown hair, brown eyes. Last seen in Fulton County, Georgia. The name wasn't right. Neither was the shape of the face or the eye color, and yet somehow Tom knew exactly who he was looking at.

And then he noticed the police report attached to the missing persons file. He saw the crime this young man was suspected of committing.

Suddenly Thomas Cross was terrified for the safety of his cousin.

Epilogue

Nearly two months went by without any further sign of trouble. The bounty hunters were apparently waiting to make another move. Raven sent no one else after them. Even The Whisper seemed to back off for a while, though they caught reports on TV of more homeless people and local vagrants found hacked to death downtown.

Christmas Eve came upon them before they knew it, and though the mood was somber after Blitz's death, it felt as though the world had given them a reprieve. The four of them made no plans to go out that night, or the following day. They would simply sit around the fireplace and enjoy each other's company.

Each of them was to receive a present from the other three. They had gotten together to decide what that present would be, and in no case was it hard to determine what should be given to whom.

They sat in the den that night - Melissa stretched out on the couch, Jason in the easy-chair, Nick sitting on the floor with his back against the leather rocking chair, Stacy also sitting on the floor close to him.

Nick stared at the fire, the same distance in his eyes that had been there for weeks. He seldom smiled now, and the others felt their hearts break a little when they would catch him going out in the afternoon to sit by his friend's grave in silence.

"Nick first," said Stacy, and Melissa pulled out a small wrapped item and tossed it to him.

It was roughly the size and shape of a small book, and when Nick unwrapped it, he discovered that his first impression was not that far off. It was a leather-bound journal, blank on the inside, waiting to be filled. On the front inside cover, embossed in gold lettering, were all four of their names.

Nick looked at them all in turn, smiling and grateful, though wondering why they had chosen to give him a journal.

"We want an insight into that tightly-shut brain of yours," Melissa answered his unspoken query. "Write about your life, your thoughts, your fears, anything you want to put on paper."

"One day, when you're ready, you can let us read it, and we'll be able to know you better," Stacy said next.

"You're a pretty hard fellow to read sometimes, bud, and it's much easier to read words than it is to read thoughts - especially yours," Jason added with a smirk.

"You're one to talk," Nick replied, and they all shared a laugh, relieved to see him brighten up a bit..

"I...don't know what to say," Nick said, looking at his gift.

"Case in point," Jason said, and they all laughed again.

"I'll do my best," Nick offered, smiling at them.

Jason's turn was next. Nick pulled out a lone, cylindrical object from under the chair behind him and handed it to Jason, who looked truly puzzled as he took it.

"Just a little encouragement for the person we all know you still are inside," Nick said to him.

Jason unwrapped the object and found that he was holding a small, extendable telescope.

It had been so very long since he had looked at the stars the way he used to every night, before Raven, and before all of this. Once upon a time, astronomy had been his favorite hobby.

Melissa remembered Jason sitting on the roof when they were all hiding at the motel, watching the sky while he doodled in his sketch pad. He had seemed so young then, so different. Now he was so hardened and scarred - but the boy they had come to love was still in there, just like Nick had said.

"Thank you. All of you. For giving me this....and for reminding me."

They shared a moment of quiet, then Nick broke in.

"Now Stacy," he said. He then looked at her. The infrequent moments of happiness Melissa and Jason had seen in him lately had been primarily when he talked to them about Stacy's present.

"Close your eyes and hold out your hand."

Stacy did so, with her palm outstretched, awaiting whatever Nick was going to give her. She was surprised, however, when instead of laying something in her palm, he slid something around her wrist - something that jingled.

"Now open them," he said.

When Stacy opened her eyes she saw that she was wearing a small, silver chain, bedecked with three silver charms. Each of the charms was a small animal.

Nick pointed at each of the charms in turn. "Me," he said, pointing at a bird-like animal with its wings outstretched above it that could only be a mythical phoenix. "Melissa," he said, pointing to a wolf, its head reared up, as if howling at the moon. "And Jason," he said, pointing at the last charm, a powerful looking bear crouched down on all fours. Each of them had picked an animal they thought represented them best.

"And you…" Nick said, his hazel-green eyes looking deep into her brown ones, his finger circled around the bracelet itself, lightly touching her skin. "are the chain that keeps us together."

Stacy looked at him for a moment, then at the others, and then started crying. She wrapped her arms around Nick and almost knocked him over with the force of her hug.

"Thank you so much," she said. Stacy got up and hugged the others nearly as forcefully as she had hugged Nick, then returned to her place on the floor beside him. She gave him one more lingering gaze of gratitude and love. She knew then that, whatever she had done, they loved her anyway, and they always would.

"Last, but not least, something I've been holding onto for far too long," said Jason, rising to his feet and pulling something from his pocket. He had told Nick and Stacy about the gift, but they hadn't seen it before now.

Melissa's jaw dropped and all her emotional guards crumbled when she saw what he was holding.

There, in Jason's hand, dangling from a thin gold chain, was the locket that Melissa had lost long, long ago. Her mother's locket.

"Jason…how…."

"Your dad's safe. Take it."

She reached out and carefully took the locket. Her fingers grasped it gingerly as if it were made of glass.

He could tell she still couldn't believe it. He figured the item might mean something to her, but this reaction was unexpected.

"This was Mom's," she said, "but she gave it to me right before she died. I kept it on me…while my dad was hitting me…while David hurt me…while I dreamed of being somewhere else."

She looked at it as if trying to determine if it was real.

"I lost it about a week before I left. I was angry and I was determined and I didn't care what I left behind…and I regretted it ever since. I guess he must have found it and put it away in case…in case…."

She did not finish her thought but instead opened up the locket. Her fingers caressed the small picture of the smiling woman within.

"Mom," Melissa sobbed.

Jason sat down beside her and held her. He felt like he was holding a little girl now instead of the strong woman he had come to love.

When Melissa's tears subsided, Jason caressed her hair.

"She was beautiful, Melissa. Even more so than I imagined."

Melissa nodded.

"Oh yes. And I loved her. I loved her so much."

"I know you did. She obviously loved you, too."

Melissa smiled and traced a finger over her own picture on the right.

"God, I was such a goofball, even back then."

"Should we be surprised?" Nick said. They all laughed quietly.

"Nah. Just a tomboy," Jason said. "Not much has changed."

She elbowed him.

"Tomboy, huh?"

"My favorite tomboy," he said, happy to be close to her.

The two of them looked at the picture of Melissa and laughed.

The picture of Melissa before the world had done its worst to her.

The picture of the little blonde girl with the crooked teeth - the crooked teeth and the red and brown dress.

Look for Book 3 of The Pull Saga:
Available 2014
http://followthepull.com/

Made in the USA
Charleston, SC
08 November 2013